'/Praise for

Elli

A Second Chance Novel

"Elli—A Second Chance Novel, is an amazing book; it's a delightful and uplifting read while it touches upon one of the most serious diseases facing us all today–cancer. The book never preaches — it entertains with wonderful humor. I recommend this book — it's simply excellent in so many ways! A keeper — not to mention that every last penny of the author's share goes on to battle cancer. Bravo!"

Heather Graham, New York Times Bestselling Author

"DeSalvo writes with warmth and wit. Her characters leap off the page and into your heart. It is a fun read where deals, dogs and disaster blend seamlessly in a fast paced story of second chances."

Cherry Adair, New York Times Bestselling Author

"Ms DeSalvo has created a family unit out of frightened and broken folks, introducing a southern crew of characters that are a true delight! This southern charmer is sure to please most readers."

InD'Tale Magazine

"This debut novel features an adorably plucky heroine, a hot Cajun hero and a cast of hysterically eccentric family members who trip over each other to chew up the scenery. DeSalvo has created some truly memorable characters, and the blog posts she uses at the beginning of each chapter to show Elli's battle with cancer are moving."

RT Bookreviews

Other Works by Tina DeSalvo
Elli
Jewell
A Second Chance in Vegas (Romantic Times: Vegas
Anthology)

Hunt for Christmas

A Second Chance Novel

Tina DeSalvo

To the darling children in my life who keep Christmas lively and incredibly fun whether they are naughty or nice...

Molly, Trip, Grey, Ollie and Cooper

I love y'all!

Chapter One

Fa La, Louisiana *(known affectionately as Fa La La)*

"It's very weird not to hear or see another human speaking or even a car passing in the distance," Edward Stein said, looking around as if he'd missed one of those things in the calm bayou waters and weeping willow trees around them at the old boat launch where he and Camille stood. "I've never experienced this before in New York, that's for sure. We could be the only two people on earth. All I see is swamp. All I hear are mosquitoes and insects buzzing." Her colleague and -not quite- boyfriend swatted his hands into the air in front of him and dodged his head at the bugs that seemed to be drawn to him as if he was coated in sugar.

Bringing Edward home with her for Christmas was a mistake.

Coming home was not. It was time. Past time.

Camille Comeaux may have tried lying to herself that she was only returning home to Fa La La because it was Christmastime and the small community where she grew up and where her family still lived, needed help with its annual *Cajun Christmas on the Bayou Celebration*. True, it was a huge event, critically important to the community because it financially supported them for an entire year, but those weren't the reasons she'd come back.

She'd come home because she missed it. She missed her family, even if they were pushy and prone to interfering in her personal life. It had always been easier to go along with what they wanted for her than to figure out what she'd wanted for herself. A truth she wasn't proud of. A truth that she'd painfully discovered when she'd overheard her papa speaking to her mother. He'd said that Camille didn't know what the hell she wanted and that he wondered if something was wrong with her for losing the man they all thought she would marry. That conversation had chased her away with hopes that distance would force her to get the kind of backbone in her personal life that she had in professional life.

Only, she hadn't really lost Ben Bienvenu. Their relationship, which everyone expected to end with a wedding march and I-do's, was just a fantasy. Neither of them had wanted it, not really. It took her leaving Cane and Fa La La to figure that out.

Still, it felt like a rejection...a jilting. Not by Ben, but by the people in Fa La La, especially her papa. She couldn't land the man they all believed was her soul mate. Her papa had said some hurtful things about her that day as she stood in the hallway of her parents' small home, including how she'd been too cold, too hard and too self-centered with Ben. His words had cut deep inside of her. He was wrong about what he'd said but what hurt worst of all, was that he'd thought of her that way. She hadn't lived up to the expectations of her papa-the man she adored and loved beyond boundaries.

Now, as she was returning home, she felt stronger and more confident in who she was and what she wanted. Just as she had planned when she left Fa La La. Still she was hurt by her papa's words. She wouldn't let him know it and would pretend she hadn't heard them. Edward would provide some insulation. It was why she'd agreed to bring him. Well, that and he'd asked to come. She had no doubt a large part of the reason he wanted to join her was because he was curious about her remote childhood home that was only accessible by boat ride from Cane, Louisiana.

The weathered cypress planks of the boat launch wharf creaked under their feet when for the umpteenth time, Edward slapped at something that landed on his arm.

"Was that a sparrow or a mosquito?" he asked, looking at her over the top of his designer black-framed glasses. "It bit me through my shirt. I thought they weren't so active this time of year."

"That would be true if it was cold or windy, neither of which is the case this afternoon. Seventy-eight and clear." *Yeah, it was definitely a mistake bringing Edward. He'll be obsessing over the mosquitoes for the entire time we're here. Geez, wait until he sees the banana spiders.*

"That shirt is what attracts them." Camille kept the impatience out of her voice. "Mosquitoes love dark colors, especially the dark blue of your Burberry shirt."

"All I brought are dark clothes."

"That's because you were born and raised in Manhattan. Dark clothes are your calling card," she said teasingly, earning a frown from Edward. He might not have much of a sense of humor, but he was one of the most dedicated doctors in the Bellevue ER where she'd worked alongside him as an emergency room physician for the last year. And he'd been a good friend to her, helping a bayou doctor adjust to city life. He'd filled some excruciatingly lonely times, making her feel wanted again. Normal.

Edward slapped at his arm again. "What the hell? I swear, that was a bird with teeth."

Camille laughed. "We grow them big out here on the bayou. They particularly like city-folks' blood. You know, it's like if you eat chicken all the time, you want to eat steak from time to time." Edward fastened the button on his collar and zipped up his black Gucci jacket.

A horn blew from behind them and they turned around to see who it was. "You're kidding me, right?" he said, as the hot pink truck belonging to Cane's favorite, most eccentric citizen stopped where the wharf met the shell-covered parking lot.

"That's Tante Izzy." She smiled and waved. She was hoping to see her this trip. Tante Izzy was such a wise, loving, and straight-talking woman...as well as Ben's old-maid, elderly aunt. Not being part of her family was one of the hardest things about Camille and Ben not being together. "If Cane had a Queen Mother, it would be Tante Izzy." She laughed. "Oh, and look, Madame Eleanor is with her. She's Cane's version of Dr. Quinn, Medicine Woman. She's a Traiteur—a Cajun healer."

She rushed to the truck and Edward followed. When she reached the driver's side, she opened the door and hugged Tante Izzy. The truck jumped forward, and Tante Izzy slammed her heavily pink-sequined tennis shoe on the thick block strapped to the brake, there because she was so tiny she couldn't reach it otherwise.

"Put it in park," Edward said, earning a frown from both Tante Izzy and Madame Eleanor, who not only shared similar disapproving expressions, they both wore similar cotton dresses with aprons over them. Tante Izzy's were pink, of course, while Madame Eleanor wore a blue-gray color that matched both of the eighty-plus-year-old ladies' hair. The similarities between the two ended there. While Tante Izzy was small-boned and thin, Madame Eleanor was a large woman whose big bosoms rested on her even larger belly.

"Who'z dat bossy man?" Tante Izzy put her truck in park. Turning her attention to Edward, she asked, "Who'z youz daddy?"

Camille laughed and looked at Edward. "That's a question a lot of locals ask when they meet someone they don't recognize and are trying to place which family they belong to," she told him. "Tante Izzy, this is my friend, Edward Stein, he works with me in New York." Tante Izzy shook the hand he extended to her.

"Stein ain't no local name, dat's for sure." She harrumphed and looked at him from head to toe. "Da mosquitoes are goin' to eat youz up."

"So I've discovered."

"It's good to see you, Madame Eleanor," Camille said, speaking Cajun French, surprising Edward. Eleanor nodded.

"He'z a doctor too?" Tante Izzy asked, also in Cajun French.

"*Oui*." Both ladies leaned forward in unison to look at him.

"I gotz da warts and love potions, youz can treat da rest," she told Edward in English.

"Oh...Okay, you have a deal." He smiled and Eleanor sat back in her seat.

"It'z her bread and butter," Tante Izzy said, then lowered her voice to speak to Camille in French. "It'z a good thing youz here, little Camille. Fa La La needs help wit it'z problem. Dey might as well have been nailing Jell-O to da wall wit how dey are tryin to fix it."

"What problem?" Camille asked, in French, worry making her voice raspy.

"Let her people tell her," Eleanor said, also in French.

"No. Tell me what's wrong, Tante Izzy."

"I'ze don't go against my Traiteur. She helps me wit my ar-thi-ritis." She pointed to the backseat. "Take dat for youz momma. When she tole me you were comin' now, we hurried up to stop here on our way to da rosary before da weekday mass. We made pecan pralines with sugar I got from da local sugar cane mill. It'z for y'all to sell at da Fa La La Cajun Bayou Christmas."

"Dey came out real good," Eleanor added as Camille opened the back door and retrieved the box. It smelled like toasty pecans, vanilla, and creamy goodness. She handed the heavy box to Edward and closed both the back and front truck doors.

"Thank you. I'm sure they'll sell out fast."

"Of course dey will," Tante Izzy said and drove off.

As they returned to the wharf to wait for her papa, she wondered what problem Tante Izzy was talking about. No one from her family had ever mentioned any concerns with the Christmas Celebration. Before she could give it another thought, she heard her papa's boat in the distance. "That's him." She shaded her eyes to the bright sun.

"How can you tell? He's far off."

"I know that old outboard motor when I hear it. Bummbummbumm, pop. He's in his twenty-foot crabbing boat." She clapped her hands. Excitement and nerves made her heart race. *God, please don't let me see any of his awful words in his eyes. I can forget those words and move forward as if it never happened if I don't see them in his eyes.* She walked to the edge of the dock and waved as he approached and slowed the engine.

"He's not in a hurry, is he?"

"Idle zone." She saw her papa's big welcoming wave. "Remember I told you, everyone's in idle zone here. Things move at a very different pace on the bayou."

Edward slapped his cheek where an enterprising mosquito found uncovered flesh. "Damn it. The mosquitoes are more vicious than the gangs that come into the ER on a Saturday night."

"Toss me the line," Camille shouted to her papa, whose smile was as sunny as the early afternoon sky. She blew out the breath she didn't realize she was holding. He looked happy. Happy to see her. His bright smile didn't dim as he maneuvered his old wooden boat alongside the dock. She caught the line on the first toss, tied it to one of the pilings, and their differences and time apart slid away.

She stepped onto the boat. It bobbed in the shallow water, but her legs were as steady as they ever were. She threw herself into her father's arms. "Oh, Papa." Just those two words caught in her throat and the tears came instantly. "I've missed you."

He kissed the top of her head, his rough beard catching in her dark strands. His hair was once the same coal color as hers before gray started marking his years ago. It seemed there was more since she last saw him.

"My little *bebette*," her papa said, his Cajun accent as thick and beautiful as ever. "I knew youz wouldn't stay away for Christmas. I'm happy youz here." He tightened his arms around her and she felt warmth and love in his embrace.

"No Papa. I came home for Christmas."

"Thanksgiving," Edward said to Camille. "We're here for Thanksgiving." She didn't bother telling him that in Fa La La, Christmas began with Thanksgiving.

Her papa looked at him over Camille's head, which was easy enough for him to do, since he was a good foot taller than her petite five foot two inches. *"Il est un couillon."* Camille covered her laugh, hearing her papa refer to one of the top ER physicians in New York as a fool.

"I've missed you." She rested her cheek on the soft, worn denim overalls covering his chest and inhaled deeply. He smelled of fresh air, Dial soap, his favorite Juicy Fruit gum, and home before she'd heard his terrible words. She could've stayed right there in his tight embrace, but Edward cleared his throat, reminding her he was there too.

She turned and waved to him to join them. He looked at her papa. "Permission to come on board, Captain." He smiled, proud of himself for using the maritime formality he'd obviously researched so he'd behave appropriately. It was both sweet and annoying.

Her papa mumbled under his breath, clearly finding it just annoying. "Papa, I'd like to introduce you to my friend, Dr. Edward Stein. Edward, this is my father, Dudley Comeaux."

"Mr. Comeaux, it's a pleasure to meet you. Camille has told me so much about you."

"She ain't told me nothing about you," he mumbled, taking Edward's hand. "Call me T-Dud."

Edward nodded. "Permission to come aboard, Captain T-Dud."

"*Mais,* get your ass on da boat, Stein, and stop all dat two-stepping youz doing."

"Mosquitoes," Edward said, as if that explained his swaying and swatting dance. Without another word, he leaped like a hurdler onto the boat. Camille sucked in a breath and rushed toward him.

Dear Lord, what does he think he's doing?

Before she could grab him by the arm, the boat dipped and jerked forward under his weight and momentum, then halted abruptly because it was tied to the piling. It slid back. Edward's body couldn't keep up and he flipped back.

 She didn't know how he did it, but Edward ended up facedown, his arms spread-eagle and gripping the sides of the boat. One foot had hooked onto a life vest tucked into the sidewall, preventing him from going over. Camille stood in wide-eyed-shock a full three seconds as she looked at him to make sure all of his bones were in the right place—which they were. She started to move to help him, but Edward held up a hand and waved her away.

Her papa rolled his eyes. "Stein, youz act like a drunk duck stepping on a banana peel."

He forced a smile as he slowly rolled onto his back and made his way to sit on the big ice chest at the back of the boat. Camille quickly turned her back to Edward because her papa's comment had made her smile and she didn't want to make him feel any worse than he already did. God, she'd forgotten how much she enjoyed her papa's sense of humor. That's because she knew the good and caring man who teased and joked with family and friends. How long would it take Edward to recognize that too? By the way he was frowning, she suspected it might take a while.

When Camille and her papa had the two suitcases and pralines on board and the boat untied, he looked at

Edward. "Now, youz hold on tight. We don't want youz to fall overboard and get eaten by da gators before da family gets to meet you."

Papa started the engine and they began their twenty-minute ride from Cane to Fa La La.

Camille was coming home.

***

Hunt sat on a slanted old rocking chair on the slanted old front porch of a slanted old cypress cabin on a quiet eleven-acre island that he owned in the middle of the Louisiana bayous and sighed. He was a happy man.

These uncivilized, watery wilds suited him – from the guttural sound of the gators, the hoot of owls, the flop of leaping fish, to the various sounds of all the other wild creatures that inhabited the fragile south Louisiana wetlands, cypress forest, and intruding saltwater marsh. What didn't suit him were his noisy neighbors across the expansive bayou off the eastern side of his paradise island. They were why he was building his new home on the western side of the island.

The door squeaked behind him as it was pushed open on rusty hinges that needed to be replaced. "That was a productive phone call with the window manufacturer," his longtime friend and home contractor, Luke Marcelle, told him. He handed Hunt a cold longneck beer. "I got them to drop their price by thirty-two percent for those hurricane impact, energy-rated, and noise-reduction windows you want for your dream home."

"Saving money is good. You're good. That's why I've put the construction of my home in your capable hands." He took a draw of his beer. It fizzed on his tongue, feeling cold and tangy. "But you do know if it's a choice between saving thirty-two percent and getting my home built by our tight deadline...I choose getting my house built on time."

"You can count on me making the deadline and you handing me my hefty bonus."

Dream home. That's exactly what his island and the house he'd designed to put on it was. He'd wanted a quiet place to retreat to when he wasn't off photographing the worst and best of Mother Nature and man. The solitude he needed to recover from his emotionally and physically draining work had to come with the convenience of power, water, and cell-phone service though. He wanted isolation, not discomfort. So that was what he'd sought in his Internet searches of secluded property for sale. Had Hunt known when he found this island that it was so close to the Cajun community of Fa La La, he probably wouldn't have bought it. But he had, with the real estate photos and description closing the deal.

Hunt was not such a curmudgeon that he didn't appreciate the uniqueness of the neighboring island-town built over water and marsh grass. With its cypress buildings on stilts and maze of walkways connecting them, it was all that remained of what once was a Native American settlement. Why did it have to be two hundred feet from his island?

Having the Fa La La small mercantile nearby was convenient, he'd admit, when he needed bread or other supplies in a hurry. The next nearest store was a twenty-minute boat ride and then another ten-minute car ride away.

"There seems to be a different energy today," Hunt said, motioning to Fa La La. "People are moving about more, smiling more."

"Yeah? I hadn't noticed." Luke took a drink of his beer and checked e-mail on his phone.

"Of course you didn't. There are no backhoes or blueprints involved."

Luke laughed. "Other than a long-legged, friendly woman, what else is there to concern yourself with in this world?" He lifted his beer to toast Hunt, who returned the gesture, although aside from a friendly woman, Hunt pretty much disagreed with his friend. "Maybe it's just because they're preparing for Thanksgiving tomorrow."

Hunt looked at Luke. "Thanksgiving? Tomorrow?"

"Man, you need to get out from behind your camera lens and walk into a Wal-Mart. There's no mistaking the holiday there."

"Maybe if you had a turkey defrosting in the sink, I would've known." Luke snorted at Hunt's comment. "There's no mistaking Christmas is coming around here." Hunt's words felt bitter on his tongue. "I just hadn't realized it was tomorrow."

And since tomorrow was Thanksgiving, that meant the Fa La La *Cajun Christmas on the Bayou Celebration* was opening tomorrow. He'd gotten a hard dose of reality of what that would sound and look like around his remote island. The past few nights, the people of Fa La La had tested the cheery Cajun holiday music, multicolored twinkling lights, large animated reindeer, alligators, and red-stocking-hat-wearing raccoon figures. There were more Christmas lights strung along the hundreds of feet of walkways, over every tin roof in the village, along every inch of wooden dock, and on practically every floating vessel, than Santa's elves put up at the North Pole. And he didn't like it. Not by his peaceful island.

Hunt felt like he was caught in a Dr. Seuss Christmas book nightmare. He had a strong urge to play the Grinch and sneak into the Fa La La village and steal Christmas.

The sound of an approaching motorboat made him frown. *Get used to it, buddy,* he warned himself. Starting tomorrow at dusk, there were going to be a lot of boats floating by. At least this one just held three people. He lifted his camera, enjoying the extra weight from the telephoto lens that he'd put on his favorite camera. This time it was trained on two of the three people climbing out onto the dock. A man and a woman. He recognized the big man still on the boat, even without his camera. T-Dud Comeaux. He and a half dozen of the Fa La La leaders had come to his island a month ago, and twice a week ever since, trying to talk him into opening his island to the Christmas pageantry. He'd explained to them that this island was now a construction site and soon to be his private home. It was no longer the Cypress Island they'd once used as part of their Christmas festivities.

The man with the casual black jacket and Buddy Holly glasses tripped on the last step from the lower dock to the upper platform. The tiny woman behind him caught him under his arms. Her midnight-colored hair swung away from her tiny waist as she leaned back, waiting for him to get his balance. Maybe he needed to get new glasses.

Hunt zoomed in on the woman with the dark, silky hair.He started focusing on her face as she turned to speak to T-Dud who'd just come up behind her, two steps lower, making them practically the same height. Blue eyes, he noticed first. The clarity of his sophisticated camera lens allowed him to see her eyes were the brilliant, almost iridescent color of the blue morpho butterfly that he'd photographed once while on assignment in the Amazon. Her eyes crinkled as she said spoke to T-Dud. Hunt widened the shot, just slightly, to see the rest of her face, almost afraid that he'd be disappointed.

He wasn't.

Her mouth, unadorned with lipstick, was full, pink, and smiling over straight white teeth. Her cheekbones were high and her chin small but well formed. She looked like a fairy-tale princess.

She turned and went up the last step and was embraced by T-Dud's wife, who had the same near-black hair color, only cropped much shorter. He'd met June in the mercantile, where she worked. She had the same fair complexion and petite frame too. Aunt? Mother? By the length and intensity of the hug, he guessed mother. As the younger woman embraced the other people there, the man who'd had to be rescued by this fairy princess stood at the back of the crowd, scratching his face.

Hunt watched the welcoming party for a few minutes more, until one of the older men, one he'd seen in the mercantile every time he went there, pointed toward his island. The fairy princess's smile faded as she turned to look in his direction. She shaded her eyes with her hand. Still holding his camera with one hand, he waved to her with the other. It wasn't meant to be friendly or adversarial. It just was an acknowledgment that he knew she was looking at him. Then, to his surprise, she ran down the steps, boarded the boat she'd arrived on, and headed to his island.

His afternoon was about to get interesting.

Chapter Two

Camille realized she'd left Edward at Fa La La when she was about halfway across Bayou Soliele. Too late to go back. She took her phone from her back jeans pocket and texted him. *I'm sorry for rudely running off without making sure you were settled and comfortable with my family. I'll be back soon.*

His response was- *okay.* She had no idea if that was an angry or an understanding okay.

She'd explain to him how hearing about what was happening to her family made her feel the same as she did when a critical patient was rushed into the ER. She had to take care of the emergency and fix it right away. Her focus was on the injured, nothing else.

What was most important right now was getting the Fa La La *Cajun Christmas on the Bayou Celebration* back on Cypress Island. She had only three minutes to devise a strategy to make that happen. There was no other place to move it to with enough land in close proximity to Fa La La to have the activities they'd held on that island for so long.

Maybe at one time there was, but not anymore.

Coastal erosion was destroying the swamp and land in coastal Louisiana. The solid marsh that had once surrounded Fa La La was gone now. Cypress Island remained, and thrived, because of its unique location in relation to tidal currents and sediment deposits – and because it hadn't been affected by cut-through canals created by the oil industry. It had been a perfect place two generations ago and it was a perfect place now for the Christmas activities that wouldn't fit on the stilted island-village.

Practicing emergency medicine had honed Camille's skills when it came to thinking and responding quickly. The problem was that she had no information with which to formulate a plan for this situation. She had no idea who the new owner was or what motivated him. All she knew was what her grand-papa had said about him, that he was as stubborn as a barnacle on an old oyster boat.

A barnacle that is going to ruin Christmas for all of us.

By the time Camille docked the boat alongside the floating wharf that looked like it had been constructed within the last month, she'd decided that all she could do was be direct with him, like she would be with an obstinate patient.

She looked toward the porch where two men sat. Which was owner and which was companion? They looked to be about th=]e same age, early thirties, and both men had dark hair and wore long sleeve T-shirts. The one with the camera had hair a little darker, longer, and wavier than the other. His T-shirt was tan with no imprint on it and the other's was light blue with something she couldn't decipher across the front. Both men, as far as she was concerned, were not very friendly.

"You could get off your lazy butts and greet your visitor properly. Invited or uninvited, it's what you're supposed to do," she mumbled as she secured the boat to one of the new pilings. "If you want to live around here, try acting like the people who live around here."

Walking toward the weather-worn cabin, she noticed that the paint on the half-dozen rows of cypress knees edging the island on both sides of the wharf had faded and was in need of refreshing. The eight families of Fa La La took a lot of pride in repainting the cypress knees each year with the Christmas characters that visitors looked forward to seeing. That was just one of the things she needed to explain to him.

"Good afternoon," she said when she reached the uneven steps to the cabin. The man holding the camera just stared at her, while the other man smiled and stood. He extended his hand.

"Hi. I'm Luke Marcelle and this antisocial man is Hunter James."

Camille shook his hand and didn't bother extending her hand to Hunter James. His piercing dark brown eyes told her that he wouldn't shake it. "I'm Camille Comeaux." He blinked, shifted in the rocker. Clearly there was recognition. Had she met him before? She didn't think so. She would've remembered his square jaw, smooth olive complexion, and piercing brown eyes.

"The prodigal doctor has returned," Hunter said, putting his camera on the upturned barrel being used as a side table. Two empty beer bottles were on it too. He glanced at Luke. "She's T-Dud's daughter."

Luke nodded.

"The people of Fa La La enjoy talking about family," she said, keeping her tone friendly. "I'm guessing you're the new owner of Cypress Island."

"He is," Luke said, smiling. "I'm just the lowly carpenter working for him."

"Actually, he's my contractor who's leaving to make sure my windows get ordered." Luke saluted Camille and walked into what she knew, from when Mr. Gaudet owned it, was a four-room cabin—a kitchen and living room combo, two bedrooms, and a small bathroom. Because it didn't look like any repairs had been done to the outside of the rusty, tin-roofed cabin, she imagined it still had the same pine vertical paneling and dull terra-cotta-colored linoleum floor inside.

"Have a seat, Doc." He pointed to the rocker that Luke had vacated. "Say your piece. I can see it in your anxious, studious baby blues that you want to."

She climbed the steps and sat in the old rocker that was leaning toward Hunter's because of the awkward slope of the porch. She looked out toward the bayou and Fa La La. It was a point of view that she hadn't had in a long time. "I swear those cypress trees have grown another ten feet since I was here last." She compared their heights to that of the houses and buildings at Fa La La that were built on twelve-foot pilings. "They must be fifty or sixty feet."

"How about that," Hunt said, looking at her and not the cypresses. She knew he was trying to get her measure, so she wasn't overly uncomfortable that he was staring at her.

"I'm glad to see they haven't lost their leaves yet." She inhaled the clean air, sweetened by the freshly cut lawn around the cabin and the verdant cypresses, wind-sculpted water oaks behind them, and the knee-high marsh grass edging the island. "The birds love these trees." She pointed to the umbrella-like tops of the cypresses and the bright green leaves on straight branches that provided refuge to the dozens of white egrets perched there. She glanced at him. "As I'm sure you know. Have you seen any of the migratory birds flying south for the winter yet?"

"Some. I saw some geese and ducks."

She smiled, but had yet to get one back from him. "In April it's even better. That's when you get the neotropical birds through here. If you get lucky, you may even see some that are as colorful as rainbows." She looked away from the towering trees. "I'm sorry if I'm rambling. I just love it here, and I want everyone to see it as I do."

"Interesting enough conversation," he offered. "But I know you're here for reasons other than to talk about trees and birds." He motioned with his head toward Fa La La, where a half dozen people had gathered on the main level walkway facing them.

She laughed. "For the record, I'm here on my own account."

Hunt extended his long legs in front of him as if to tell her that he was totally comfortable in his own skin and she didn't intimidate him one bit. The fact that his narrow feet were clean and bare and the hems of his faded jeans were as frayed as the fabric over his knees told her that he wasn't a man worried about impressing others either.

He did seem to care about his body, she noted. He had wide, broad shoulders that tapered to narrow hips. She imagined that his flat stomach would be firm and toned. Whether he worked to achieve that lean, healthy body because of vanity, the pleasure of working out, or for necessity because his job required it, she didn't know. She also didn't know why, when she'd seen thousands of male bodies before, his made her pulse increase. Maybe it was because he wasn't on an examining table and she wasn't his doctor.

"I need to talk to you about the Fa La La *Cajun Christmas on the Bayou Celebration*," she said, shifting in the rocker to fully face him.

He stood, walked down the stairs and sat on the second step.

Dear Lord. How do I have a serious discussion with him when he's a moving target? She promptly followed him down the steps and stood nearby. "Your island is important to the success of the celebration."

His response was to pick up a pair of running shoes, knocking them upside down against one another, before putting them on his bare feet.

She moved to stand directly in front of him. "It's quite a serious matter." He looked at her tapping foot and smiled. Heat rushed into her cheeks. She hadn't even realized she was doing it. She pressed her foot soundly to the ground.

"You're wound up with too much energy, Doc." He tied his shoes in a slow easy manner. "Let's go for a walk." He stood.

She joined him as he started to walk away. Her phone dinged in her back pocket as she reached Hunter's side. She read her text – it was from Edward. *Do you want me to come to the island to assist you?*

Her phone dinged again. Another text. It was from her mother: *Don't let Edward go to the island. You'll have a better chance to convince Hunt to change his mind if it's just the two of you. We've met him. He's safe. You won't need your papa's gun from the boat just in case you were thinking about that. Don't forget to finger-comb your hair.*

And then there was a third text from her older sister, Sarah: *He's really handsome. Smile a lot and don't shoot him.*

She'd been home for less than an hour and her family was already trying to tell her what to do and play matchmaker. Both reasons why she'd left in the first place.

"Are we going to walk and enjoy nature or are you going to stay on that phone and ignore it?" Hunter said, frowning.

"I need to change out of my loafers." She motioned to the boat. Hunt, as her mother called him, followed her to the wharf. She put on her mother's white rubber boots that were kept in the boat for when she went crabbing with Papa. Since she and her mother were about the same size, they slipped on easily. She lifted her phone to show Hunt and then put it in the storage space under the seat. She looked at the gun her papa kept there and rolled her eyes, thinking about what her momma texted. Insanity. She shook her head and met him back on land.

"You've been away too long," he said as they started their slow stroll toward the center of the island. "You should shake your shoes and boots to make sure no spiders have crawled inside."

She smiled. "I looked, but you're right. Shaking exposed shoes is much better. I can't even begin to tell you how many spider bites on toes and feet I've treated. Caterpillars too, for the same reason." She looked at him, shading her eyes with her hand. "Where are we going and why are we going there?"

He shrugged. "Have you really been away for over a year?"

She sighed, nodded. "Yeah. I had things to do." The sweet scented green lawn gave way to thick patches of fall marsh grass that were connected by the heavy clay mud of coastal Louisiana. The mud was dry and firm under their feet. Its heavy musty odor, which changed with tides and season, was released with every step they took.

"There are always things to do." His tone was more of understanding than mocking. "I wonder what things you had to do, Doc. I wonder if you still feel like you have other things to do too."

"There are always things to do," she repeated his words. He laughed softly. "I have a thing to do right now," she said, directing the conversation to the purpose of her visit.

"To discuss the over commercialization of Christmas?"

"To discuss the under-appreciation of tradition," she replied.

He laughed again, reaching for her hand to help her cross a small heavily vegetated stream. That simple, harmless gesture made her flesh rise with chill bumps while the hand he still held filled with an unexpected warmth. There were no medical or physiological reasons that should happen. She removed her hand from his.

"You have my undivided attention, Doc. Tell me why I'm under-appreciating tradition."

"I'd be happy to." She stopped walking and reached for his arm. Once again, she felt a jolt of heat where her hand touched him. Did he feel it too? When he stopped, she lifted her hand and tested the temperature against her forehead.

"Feeling feverish?" There was amusement, not concern, in his eyes and his easy grin. What did he know about her rapid pulse and oddly elevated temperature sensations?

She dropped her hand. "No. I feel fine. I just haven't acclimated to the warmer temps and higher humidity here compared to New York." He folded his arms over his chest and waited for her to speak again. "Traditions," she said, as a reminder to him and herself. Now her face was beginning to feel flushed with his rich, coffee-brown, perceptive eyes so focused on her. She knew, in a way she couldn't explain, that this man saw things with more insight than others did. "This Christmas celebration is a tradition for the people of Fa La La and all of the families who travel here year after year to enjoy it."

"Is it really a tradition or is it economy?"

"Both," she said honestly. "Just like shrimping, crabbing, and hunting are economy for the people of Fa La La, it's also part of their...our tradition. We've been living off the land since the first Houmas Indian families settled in this area in the seventeen hundreds. This Christmas celebration is just another way to live off the land and follow our traditions. We gather together to make moss and palmetto wreaths, to bake homemade cookies with recipes passed down from generation to generation."

Oh, the cookies, Camille thought, surprised that the scent of pure vanilla extract, heavy cane sugar, and dry flour seemed to drift from her memory into the air. So did the vision of how they would lay freshly bleached sheets on the beds and place the cookies there after they'd come out of the oven. She felt the same excitement within her as she had when she was a child. She'd forgotten how much she loved baking cookies with her family.

She cleared her throat, which had suddenly become dry with emotion. She smiled. "We've been working together and putting the Cajun Bayou Christmas Celebration on out here for a hundred years."

"Not always, in the way it was described to me," he said, sounding annoyed. "You can't tell me that a hundred, even forty years ago, Fa La La celebrated Christmas for a full month."

No. She couldn't say that at all. That started in the mid 1980s when she was eight years old. It would serve no purpose to tell him that, though. "Why are you against us sharing our Indian and Cajun traditions and cultures during the Christmas season?"

"I'm not really." He tucked his hands into his pocket. "I'm not particularly fond of it happening so close to my quiet sanctuary, but I know I can't stop it. But I can stop it from happening *on* my island."

"Your island. Can anyone really own property or even the sky and the earth?" She glanced at him to see if he was buying any of what she was saying. He just stared at her like he was listening intently, so she continued. "Indians believed that the land is our mother nourishing all..."

Hunt laughed aloud. "Really, Doc? Is that the best argument you have? Massasoit philosophy about no man having ownership of Mother Earth? It's a nice idea from an Indian tribal leader from Rhode Island in the 1600s. I live in the modern world where real estate transactions occur – you know, where I purchase a parcel of land from another person who has the ownership deed to it."

He laughed again and because she'd been totally ridiculous going there, she laughed too. Yeah. It was a desperate move from a woman who wanted to help and please her family.

"Okay." She held up her hands. "It just shows you how eager I am to get you to change your mind."

"How eager are you?" His voice dropped an octave. His pupils dilated as he looked at her mouth.

She rolled her eyes and started to walk away. "Not that eager. Now who's being ridiculous? At least my Mother Earth philosophy spiel didn't involve the exchange of body fluids with a stranger."

He walked alongside her. "Why is this island so important for the celebration? So you can show off cypress knees painted with Santa and Mrs. Claus? So you can roast marshmallows and paint a few kids' faces? What does that have to do with tradition?"

"It has everything to do with helping sustain a way of life that will be lost if the people here can't afford to stay." She stopped and faced him. "Why do you object to letting us come on your island, having a lovely bonfire, some live reindeer for the children to feed, and a lover's path for couples? We won't harm the island in any way."

He turned to face her. "Doc, this is a construction site. I'm building my home here." He pointed ahead of them through a clearing where a floor and walls had been constructed on top of twelve-foot pilings. "Let your Christmas revelers go to the zoo and pet reindeer there. Let dreamy-eyed couples stroll on someone else's property, and let them have bonfires in their own backyards. Not my island. This is my home."

"Hunter. Let's find a compromise."

He gripped her by her shoulders, his fingers digging into her flesh. "No compromise. I need my peace. I need my privacy. Why else would a man build a home in the middle of a Louisiana swamp?" He let her go.

She gripped him above his elbows, where she could reach him with their height difference. She let her fingers bite as hard as his had. "This is too important for me to just give up because you try some masculine intimidation. I don't intimidate easily. I've faced more dangerous men than you. Don't think that because you want your privacy we can't find an agreeable compromise."

She released his arms and he smiled. She felt like slapping that smile off his arrogantly handsome face. She looked away, needing to cool her temper. She had to be smarter and more in control of her feelings if she wanted to save Fa La La. She thought of baking Christmas sugar cookies with pecans and painting cypress knees like sweet angels. She faced Hunt again.

"You need to know the people you're drawing the line in the sand with, Hunt. My people. Your neighbors. Join us for Thanksgiving tomorrow. You and Luke. Come around eleven-thirty. We eat at noon." She looked up at a single graceful white egret that flew low over them, with the cypress tree branches draped in moss behind it. "This is a beautiful, peaceful island."

She walked away. As she boarded the boat to go back to Fa La La, she wondered what in the hell kind of compromise she could come up with to change his mind.

Chapter Three

Garlic, onions, and the spices that made Cajun food deliciously memorable greeted Hunt as he ascended the dark, chicory-brown stairs from the dock at water level up to the main walkways. He paused, looking around at the maze of eight-foot-wide boardwalks that were sturdily trussed over the bayou and marsh grass below. They passed in front of dozens of clean, weathered cypress board buildings topped with tin roofs. He had no idea where he was supposed to go from here to find Camille or the Thanksgiving meal she'd invited him to attend...and he'd accepted because he was curious. The beautiful Dr. Camille had piqued his curiosity about her and the people of Fa La La.

Curiosity was what drove him to capture photos in the most challenging situations. It wasn't much different, he supposed, coming into this unique community where he was not the most favored neighbor – even though he was their only neighbor.

The mercantile. He'd start at the one place he'd been before and see what happened. Shifting his well-used camera backpack on his shoulder and a bottle of California white wine in his hand, he headed to the Comeaux family store. It only took about fifteen seconds to reach it and the *Store Closed* sign on the front door. Hunt paused and inhaled deeply, enjoying the warm late morning air filling his lungs and the incredible scents from the meal prep not too far away. Of course in this small settlement, nothing was very far away.

He listened for a moment. There was distant laughter, pots clanging, water running...and Camille's voice. She was asking someone nearby if she'd made enough potato salad. It was coming from one building over. Hunt moved toward her voice.

Rock music played from somewhere, far enough away that he could only make out the beat as he walked under the tall awning, covering the distance from the mercantile to the next building twenty-four feet away. That building, he assumed was the home of T-Dud and June. Come rain or shine, they'd be protected by the sturdy tin roof from home to work. Only a few other places that he could see, had covered awnings protecting the eight-foot wide walkway. He raised his hand to knock on the door.

"Dere you are," T-Dud said, coming from between the buildings and handing Hunt a can of beer. He put his heavy, beefy arm over Hunt's shoulder and directed him down a walkway leading toward the back of the building that he'd heard Camille's voice coming from. "We're frying up da turduckens out here," T-Dud said. "Wit what's cooking outside and wit da gumbo and oyster dressing cooking inside, a man will think he'z died and gone to heaven. Sure smells good, huh?"

Hunt's stomach growled. "There's your answer." He laughed.

T-Dud chuckled, stopping as they reached the back of the building. "Look who's here," he announced to the three men sitting on two glider swings on the walkway that overlooked the bayou. It was pleasantly shaded from the bright sun by the building next to them. Even in the shade and with the light breeze, it was a warm November day.

Hunt recognized two of the men. One was T-Dud's eighty-something-year-old father, Mr. Dudley, who was always at the mercantile whenever he went in. He was sitting next to the Buddy Holly eyeglasses guy who had arrived yesterday with Camille. Today he was dressed in black slacks and a black button-down shirt. Maybe he was the local priest. The other man, who wore jeans, red suspenders, and a blue plaid shirt, he'd never seen before. He'd have remembered him by his long gray and strawberry-blond ponytail. T-Dud and Mr. Dudley both wore their overall jeans with different Christmas-embroidered collared shirts. "Youz know Mr. Dudley," T-Dud said, leaning against the newly painted rail wrapped in unlit Christmas lights, garland, and moss. He pointed his beer can at the strawberry blond. "Dat's Pierre." Then he nodded his head at the man in black. "And dat's Edward, Camille's friend. He works in da ER wit her in New York." Not a priest. A doctor.

Hunt put the camera bag and wine bottle on the ground to shake hands with the men. He was surprised that even Mr. Dudley made an effort to make him feel welcome, when he'd felt they tolerated him at best while he was shopping at the mercantile. They'd been friendly enough when they first came over to plead their case on the island, but with each subsequent visit their impatience and annoyance grew. He didn't blame them – they were just frustrated as hell that he was holding his ground and they didn't know how to rattle him loose. Camille must've told them to be on their best behavior so she could give it a fair try too.

They were all wasting their time.

"Is your friend coming?" Edward asked, holding his beer but not drinking it. He looked like a man who rarely drank out of anything other than glass or crystal. He also looked like a man who either was going through puberty again or was allergic to mosquito bites. Three huge, infected, raised marks on his left cheek glowed like the damn red Christmas lights on Rudolph's nose.

"Luke isn't coming," he said. "He got guilted into spending Thanksgiving with his sister in Atlanta. He flew out there this morning."

"You should be with family for the holidays," Pierre said. "Where's your family, Hunt?"

"Just me. Both my parents are deceased and I have no siblings."

They all took a drink of their beers, except Edward. "Holidays are tough without family or missing a family member who isn't with them," T-Dud said, and Hunt got the feeling it was said with sincerity for him, but also for Edward to hear too. Was he responsible for keeping Camille from home?

Hunt nodded to T-Dud. "I'm usually working during the holidays. It suits me."

"Not today," Mr. Dudley said, waving his hand in a broad gesture. "Today, youz pass a good time wit us."

"Hunt, happy Thanksgiving," Camille said as she walked out the back door of the building next to them and into a slant of sunshine. Or had she lit up the space around her with her bright smile? She was glowing. "I'm glad you decided to join us."

Her silky black hair was clipped up and back by one of those toothy plastic contraptions he'd seen women wear. It exposed how fair her complexion was along the long column of her neck, the underside of her smooth jaw, and beneath her flushed cheeks. Hunt wondered if her naked flesh would be just as flawless and creamy. Not a good thought to have with her father, grandfather, and boyfriend next to him.

As Camille greeted Pierre, Hunt got the camera from his bag and snapped a photo of her, and then the men around her. No need to let on to everyone there just how much he wanted to photograph her in that light and that space.

Laughing, she playfully posed with Pierre, then her grandfather, and Edward. "How fun. We have someone with more than a cell phone to take Thanksgiving photos. I hope you plan to share them."

"Quite a sophisticated camera for a hobbyist," Edward said when Hunt placed the camera on his lap. "What is that, a Canon?"

"Yeah," Hunt said, not feeling a need to explain that photography was more than a hobby. It was a life's passion.

Camille asked him about Luke and as he told her, he noticed she was wearing Christmas colors – holly-green leggings, a dark red turtleneck, and black leather short boots. No harvest colors or cornucopia or pumpkins for the people of Fa La La. He glanced down at his clothes. Jeans, boots, neutral tan button-down shirt. Not a single hint of Christmas.

Just the way he liked it.

"You men aren't overcooking the turducken are you?" Camille asked, looking from one man to the next.

They grunted and groaned in mock offense, but T-Dud walked to where three huge deep fryers were positioned under a hinged pulley with a rope and thick J-hook. "Five more minutes. Da turkey and duck are done, just waiting on da chicken." He laughed.

"Don't youz worry about da men," Mr. Dudley told her. "You just make sure da gumbo is ready." Hunt walked to the fryer and snapped a few photos of the amber oil roiling around the golden brown turkey. He changed the setting, hoping a little less brightness of the image would bring to mind the mouthwatering scents of the salty crispness of the skin and the sweet, tenderness of the meat. He also took a few shots of T-Dud.

"I'll let the others know they can head over to the Hall," Camille said, then turned to the bayou, where splashing could be heard. She leaned over the railing. "You boys come on up now. Dinner's just about ready." Hunt went to stand next to Camille. "Those boys are always in their pirogues fishing, frogging, or just messing around," she told him.

"Who are they?" He'd observed the five dark-haired boys, who appeared to be between thirteen and fifteen years old, from his island.

"The tall one in the middle is my brother's son, Jean. The rest are my cousins." She looked at Hunt as he took photos of the boys laughing and splashing each other with their push poles. "We're all cousins or siblings or related somehow here."

Edward moved to stand next to Camille, his shoulder touching hers. She didn't look at him and Hunt got the feeling that they did not have a passionate relationship. "One close-knit family," he said, in a tone that neither indicated that he thought it was a good or bad thing. "How can it not be when everyone lives so close to one another. Kind of like a mini Manhattan in the swamp."

"It can be too much family sometimes," she admitted, as her mother walked through the door. Hunt saw by the way the older woman's head came up and hurt was reflected in her eyes, she'd heard her daughter.

He snapped a photo of her. Then said hello and handed her the bottle of wine. She thanked him and asked everyone to go inside and help carry the prepared food to the Hall. The Hall, as Hunt discovered, was a huge four-season room in the middle of Fa La La. It was the hub of this small community, the gathering place, around which all the other buildings spread out like the spokes on a wheel. The houses, the mercantile, the couple of sheds, and the boats tied up below were all connected by the people who raised their families, worked, and played in this moss-draped swamp.

The savory smells of cooked meats, roasted vegetables, and rich vanilla and spiced desserts permeated the air. Women rushed around straightening silverware on the tables, filling glasses, and generally fussing as the men ambled in to take their seats.

Hunt hesitated at the door, not sure where he was supposed to go. The Hall boasted a big-screen television, sofas, cushy chairs, and several long tables. Enough tables to feed fifty to sixty people, he estimated. Were there that many people who lived in Fa La La?

God, he hoped not.

What he noticed most, though, were all of the Christmas decorations. Every inch of that room, as it was everywhere on Fa La La, was covered in lights, moss, evergreen, or fabric. There were signs, too, hanging on driftwood planks: Joyeaux Noel Jambalaya, Snow-Covered Beignets, Mrs. Claus Hot Chocolate, and Papa Noel Gumbo. "This is where we sell most of the food and drinks to our visitors," Camille said, when she noticed him looking at the signs. "We used to sell hot chocolate and coffee, along with the ingredients for s'mores, on the island." She smiled, but said no more about his island. "Everyone gets together each day of the Christmas celebration to prepare the food for that night. Except today. Most of the food was prepared yesterday."

As family and invited friends walked in, Camille introduced Hunt to them. Aside from many looking at one another after they greeted him, they didn't act like he was the Scrooge that kept his island off their beloved Christmas Celebration activity schedule. Many, he noticed, did have suggestions for Camille about moving back to Fa La La, staying in New York, dating a local man instead of Edward, cutting her hair, curling her hair, and having babies before she was too old. She never told them to mind their own business, as he would've. She just smiled, although he saw how it bothered her by the dullness of her eyes.

"Ayeee," T-Dud and Pierre shouted as they, along with a few of the teenage boys, carried the turduckens in on ceramic platters. Compliments were given and suggestions were made as gumbo, potato salad, oyster dressing, green beans, corn, and other family favorites were served...and eaten. Hunt was seated next to T-Dud, on his left, and Camille, on his right. June and her thirteen-year-old grandson, Jean, sat across from him. He ate, took photos, laughed, and enjoyed himself in a way he hadn't in a very long time. He didn't typically do crowds or personal gatherings unless he was behind the camera lens and he was paid to be there.

A few times, Hunt looked at Edward, sensing the man's unease. Edward tried to make conversation with Camille's elderly great-aunt and her middle-aged daughter, who were seated across from him. But there were strained lulls as each tried to find a topic that suited them both. Camille, who sat between Edward and Hunt, would jump to his rescue from time to time, but that seemed to annoy Edward more than the lull in conversation. Hunt didn't mind the quiet moments between small talk. Especially when he wasn't forced to participate. He enjoyed observing and listening best.

When he could eat no more, Hunt excused himself and walked outside, returning to one of the glider swings on the walkway. He leaned back and set the swing in motion as he looked out at the glassy brown bayou. The shadow of a black duck, flapping its wings without pause, slid over the bayou until duck and shadow disappeared from view behind a grove of cypress trees.

"Mind if I join you?" Camille asked. Hunt stopped the motion of the swing and patted the seat next to him. Once she sat, he set the swing into an easy glide again. "I ate too much." She patted her flat tummy.

"It's the thing to do for Thanksgiving." He smiled. "There were so many choices, so I didn't make any and ate it all."

Camille laughed. "Last Thanksgiving, I had swordfish over rice while on a ship in the South Pacific. I pretended I was eating turkey and rice dressing."

"Last Thanksgiving, I ate bananas, crackers, and beef jerky while I was in the Borneo rainforest." He laughed. "We weren't too far away from one another." He looked at her and her brows were furrowed as if she was trying to figure out what he was doing in the Borneo rainforest. "So what were you doing on a ship in the South Pacific?" he asked.

"Hopefully making a difference." She unfastened the clip in her hair. The strands fell like a silk curtain, the ends lifting in the early afternoon breeze. She rubbed her fingers against her scalp and sighed. "When I left here, I needed to immerse myself in work that was meaningful, with people I didn't know. So I contracted with a medical ship for three months. It sailed from one remote island to another, treating the medically underserved and neglected. It was exhausting, upsetting, and rewarding."

"I've read about those medical ships." He'd never actually come across one in his years working around the globe. "Why did you need to surround yourself with people you didn't know?"

"Long, boring story. Let's just say well-intentioned people can do things to make you want to find a new home address. At least for a little while."

"I like boring. I live on a deserted island."

She smiled, but it didn't reach her eyes. "I left here because I needed to let the dust settle a bit after a non-breakup with a man, a relationship that the entire parish thought was preordained in the stars." She waved her hand in dismissal. "I don't know why I told you that much. Like I said, boring."

"So far, I'm not bored." He rested his arm on the back of the swing. "What is a non-breakup?"

"Ah, that's where it gets a little complicated." She laughed softly, sounding resigned. "Ben and I weren't a committed couple with declarations of love. We were just the two people everyone, and I mean everyone, thought belonged together. I guess we went along with those ideas from time to time, until Ben actually found the woman of his dreams. She is a lovely person and perfectly suited for him."

"Let me guess." He leaned forward a little to look at her fair, expressive face better. "It was the talk of the town...I mean parish. You couldn't go anywhere without someone speaking to you and around you about it. And, from what I observed inside, your family took it on as a mission to right the wrongs that were done to you."

She turned a little to face him, her bright blue eyes wide. "Yeah, exactly that." She waved her hand in dismissal again and lifted her chin. She was about to change the subject. Hunt suspected, that she'd said more than she was comfortable with, especially to a man she hardly knew. "So, tell me, Hunt. Why were you in Borneo?"

"Photographing Bornean orangutans." He looked at her sideways in mock surprise. "Why? What did you think I was doing there?"

She laughed at his teasing and her blue eyes seemed to sparkle. He liked seeing that, rather than the sadness that was there moments ago. "So you're a photographer? I assume not the wedding and senior portrait kind."

"You assume correctly. I'm the 'I go where you pay me money to go' kind."

"Interesting. So you're motivated by the almighty dollar?" She stood, walked to the railing. "So." She turned to face him before continuing. "If I offer to pay you a lot of money, would you let us use your island for the Christmas Celebration?"

Hunt wanted to tell her *"hell no"* flat out, but because his belly was full, thanks to her, and because he was enjoying her company, he'd play along with her for a while. "How much?"

Her brows lifted. "How much would it take?"

"How much do you have?"

She twisted her pretty mouth, creating a dimple in her right cheek. "Not much." She sat on the glider swing again. "If Fa La La took money from what it earns each night to pay you, it would just be taking from Peter to pay Paul." She clasped her hands together. "Unless you charge us a reasonable fee or take a percentage of the island entry fee, I don't see how it'll work."

"It won't work." He folded his arms over his chest. "Unless you can figure out how your Christmas circus won't slow down the construction of my home and won't disturb my privacy, I don't think there's a resolution that'll makes us both happy." He stood and put his camera in its bag. "So. I vote to make just me happy."

Camille's cheeks flamed as pink as cotton candy. "You never had any intention to try to work things out with me, did you?"

"I never told you I would."

"You're an impossible man."

He took a step closer to her until he could smell the sweet vanilla from the bread pudding on her breath. "Camille, I like you. I think you're intriguing, pleasant to be around, and gorgeous. But I've worked too damn hard and frankly in too damn many dangerous situations to not enjoy what I have. I want my home on this beautiful remote island. That makes my island a construction zone that's too dangerous for John Q. Christmas enthusiast, Mary his wife, and his twin daughters to roast marshmallows and huddle around a pile of burning old wood."

Camille started stuttering, words of frustration and anger not coming to her. Hunt, feeling a bit of guilt for putting her in this state, while at the same time thinking she looked so damn cute in it, leaned to close the inch between them and kissed her sweet mouth. When she didn't push him away, he changed the angle and ran his tongue along the seam of her lips, enjoying the soft texture and plump fullness. He sucked ever so briefly on her bottom lip, feeling the sensuality of it deep in his belly and other places that made him male. Then he stepped back.

Camille, who had closed her eyes, opened them in a delayed look of surprise. She shoved him back another step.

"Is everything okay here?" Edward asked, walking up behind Hunt. "Camille?"

"Everything's fine." She narrowed her eyes at Hunt.

"Cami, we're about to have a final meeting about tonight's opening for the Cajun Christmas..." Her mother stopped speaking and walked to stand next to Hunt. He slid his camera bag onto his shoulder. "Oh. You're leaving. We'd hoped you'd join us for the meeting."

"No, ma'am. I have to go." He faced June. "Thank you for having me over for Thanksgiving. The food and company," he glanced at Camille, "were wonderful." He gave her a quick peck on the cheek, then kissed Camille on the cheek too. He turned and started to walk away. "Edward, watch out for those mosquitoes."

Chapter Four

It turned out that it wasn't mosquitoes that Edward had to watch out for. It was wasps. Two had found him as he walked from the mercantile to the Hall, carrying the paper napkins Camille's mother had asked him to retrieve. He was helping set up for the evening guests when he let out a howl that sounded like a wounded coon in the marsh.

"The Texían got stung by a gep," her eight-year-old niece, Molly, shouted, rushing to the boat dock where Camille had been loading the large thermoses of hot chocolate they served to the boat riders in paper cups. She knew that the Texían, the outsider, Molly was referring to was Edward.

"It's swelling really bad. Granny wants you to come quick, before he dies." Her middle sister's daughter was known to have a flair for the dramatic; it was why she got to dress as a snow princess, where there was rarely any snow, and hand out treat bags to the visiting children. Dramatic or not, Camille had heard the howl and knew Edward had been injured.

Camille ran into her parents' kitchen, where Edward had been taken. He was sitting at the kitchen table, looking from her mother to her sister, Kim, as they spoke. He was alert and healthy, albeit a bit confused, following their conversation about the worst wasp stings they had. Like her daughter, Molly, Kim was pretty animated and dramatic when she spoke of stepping on a nest of mud daubers.

"I stopped them from putting a wad of wet tobacco and toothpaste on the stings on my palm. I wasn't interested in unsupported country medicine mainlined into my body," he told Camille over the women's conversation, but they went silent after he spoke. "Not that I don't appreciate your effort," he added, trying to make up for the insult to her mother and sister. But, what about her? She felt offended by his comment too. He looked at Camille. "It hurts. I got stung twice."

Kim, who had a narrow-eyed expression of total irritation, sat up, ready to tear into Edward, but her mother touched Kim's arm to keep her from saying anything. Both women remained quiet, although their body language said they'd been offended. Camille knew they didn't say anything because they cared about her, and didn't want to cause a problem for her and the man they all thought was her boyfriend. How had she ever forgotten how loyal and considerate her family was? Why had she just focused on how overbearing and opinionated they could be?

"Actually, Edward," she said, lifting his hand and turning it over to make sure there were no other stings elsewhere on his hand. She kept her voice even and void of emotion. "Tobacco has a high alkaline composition, while toothpaste has both baking soda and glycerin that can help neutralize the venom. It's a clever use of what's around a home to treat a common injury."

Don't get angry with him because he isn't used to a different way of doing things, she reminded herself. Camille did a quick medical assessment of Edward. He was upright, breathing, and speaking mostly coherently. She went to the kitchen cabinet near the door where the medical supplies she provided were kept. Kim stood too.

"Molly and I have to finish filling the Santa's treat bags. The boys got into the box and ate half of them."

"They're going to get a lump of coal for Christmas, when Santa hears about this," Molly assured Camille as she followed her mother out of the house.

"And Molly's going to be the one to tell him about it," June added with a smile so full of grandmotherly love, Camille felt it in that womanly place that craved having children of her own.

"What are your symptoms, Edward?" she asked, carrying the medical bag to the table and opening it.

He sat completely still, his palm facing up and resting on the table. "Give me a second to assess."

"His hand is swellin' really bad," her mother said filling in the silence. "Red. Rashy."

"Localized pain. Stiffness." He moved his fingers. "Yeah, there's definitely pain."

"How's your breathing?" Camille placed the Epi-pen on the table next to him in case she needed it.

"Labored. But clear."

"You're probably just anxious. Take deep breaths and relax." She placed a single small pill on the table and took his pulse. When she finished, she slipped on the medical exam gloves from the bag. "Are you allergic to anything?"

"Other than possibly bee stings, no," Edward huffed.

"Are you having any trouble swallowing?" She handed him the pill from the table. "Any symptoms for anaphylaxis?"

He swallowed, his Adam's apple bobbing in his thin neck. Then he opened his mouth for her to examine it. "I can swallow."

"Take the pill. It's diphenhydramine. Mom, please give him a water." June rushed to the refrigerator, then handed him a bottle of water. She took it back immediately, because his hand was too swollen to open it and the other hand was holding the pill. After she removed the cap, she handed it back to Edward and he took his med.

Camille cleaned the wounds. "The stingers are still in." She took the sterilized tweezers from the medical bag and gently used them to remove the tiny stingers. "I can't tell if I got the venom sac too. Probably a moot point by the way you're having a large local reaction." She pointed to the red rash across his palm and up to his wrist.

"It hurts like a mo-fo. Can you get me an ice-pack, Mrs. Comeaux?"

"Of course." She reached into the medical supply bag, pulled out a cold pack, and squeezed it in her hands to activate it. Then she handed it to Camille.

"Thanks, Mom. You've always been a good nurse."

"I had good training." She smiled at her daughter and Camille felt a surge of love warm her chest. She and her mom had had a strained relationship for over a year now. She'd thought Camille should've fought for Ben's love when Elli had arrived in Cane after inheriting Sugar Mill planation with him.

That was only one of the things Camille and her family had disagreed on.

"Take it easy," Edward complained, as she placed a small bandage around the wound. "I will be a hell of lot more sympathetic with my patients who get stung from now on."

"Edward, I know it hurts, but you need to be brave. I'll give you a nice little sticker when we're done."

"Very funny," he smiled at her with such tenderness that she saw, in sudden burst of clarity, that he was in love with her. Dear Lord, she hadn't expected that and, she felt deep in her gut, she didn't want it.

Her dad walked into the kitchen, the screen door slamming shut behind him. He leaned over Edward's shoulder and whistled. "I sure hope you don't have to amputate dat hand, Stein," he said, sounding serious. "That's not da hand you wipe your ass wit is it?"

"I'm glad I could be the source of entertainment for the Comeaux family," Edward said, good-naturedly.

"Geps and mosquitoes sure like youz Yankee blood." Her papa looked at Camille. "Didn't youz tell him not to wear dark clothes?"

Forty-five minutes later, Camille spotted Edward inside her grand-papa's screened porch where he'd been assigned to help at "the bank" that was located there for the celebration to hand out change and count money. He was wearing a white long-sleeve T-shirt with Santa's face imprinted on it. Santa's beard and the pom-pom on his red cone hat were embellished with puffs of cotton. If the medical team at Bellevue could see him like that, they wouldn't believe it.

"Ready?" her papa asked, extending his hand to Camille. "I'm sure happy youz riding shotgun wit me tonight." She clasped her hand with his as she'd done when she was a little girl and thought he'd hung the moon and stars. She still thought he did, although no one had ever broken her heart the way he had. She shook that thought away. Tonight was not the time to think of it. It was the opening night of Fa La La *Cajun Christmas on the Bayou Celebration*.

"We couldn't have asked for better conditions," she told her papa as they headed to the Cane boat launch with the other five vessels in the Christmas armada. "The humidity is low. The stars are starting to pop out even though the sun hasn't yet set. And there's a nice cool breeze." She rested her head on her dad's chest. "Perfection."

As was their tradition, the lead vessel, decided by drawing straws, would give a single long toot of his horn. The other boats would answer with two toots. Then, everyone, boat captains and the people of Fa La La, would turn the Christmas lights on at the same time.

Pierre had won the honor of signaling the start of the celebration. His horn sounded from the boat in front of Camille and her papa. She and the other boats gave the answering call. Like magic, all of the lights went on and the Christmas music started playing. Everyone clapped and shouted with joy as another year of their holiday celebration began. Yes, it was commerce, but it was what kept their family together working for a common goal.

"Yeah. This is perfection."

"Not quite, *bebette*." He looked toward Cypress Island. It was dark and silent. There was only an amber light shining through the two small front windows of the dilapidated cabin. It looked so sad and lonely.

***

The sound of the first horn drew Hunt outside his cabin, with camera in hand. He jumped off the front porch and headed down to the water's edge in the shadows of the thick, weeping willows. More horns blasted and then the boats and the Fa La La settlement were lit up simultaneously. He captured the boats and small community on stilts in the silhouette of the setting sun and fiery coral sky. An instant later, he caught the dotted colors of the Christmas lights coming to life on the bayou and on the modest homes of Fa La La. Even to a man like himself, it looked beautiful.

Traditions. Camille's declaration that this Christmas event was about traditions echoed in his head. He imagined Mr. Dudley captaining a boat with his family aboard fifty years ago, doing the same thing T-Dud now did with his family. Which one of these boats with multicolored lights along its tall booms was his, he wondered, trying to make out the names on the bows? He zoomed in with his camera and found it on the second boat in the parade-*Miss June*. It was named after his wife.

Hunt wondered if Camille was on the boat with her father. He swallowed hard, guilt gnawing at his conscience. He didn't have to be so harsh with her. He could've chosen kinder words and an easier tone. Yet telling her that he'd never agree to letting them hold the Christmas Celebration on Cypress Island felt like much more than a rejection of her demands. It felt like he was fighting for more than his privacy.

"Help a guy out," Luke said, dragging an ice chest with two tan canvas umbrella chairs on top of it. He stopped a few feet up on the slight rise that led to the bayou.

Hunt unfolded the chairs and placed one on each side of the ice chest. He sat in the chair on the right. He opened the ice chest and took out two beers, handing one to Luke. "How's your sister?"

Luke sat and twisted the top off his beer bottle and tossed it inside the ice chest. Hunt did the same. "Nice. It's always good to see Lucy, even for a quick trip in and out in the same day. We went out to one of the downtown hotels and ate there." He waved his beer toward Fa La La. "I was hoping you'd bring leftovers back."

"My departure didn't inspire anyone to give me a care-package."

"I'm not surprised." Luke drained his beer and got another. "You know, it might cost you a few dollars, but we can put the construction on hold for the duration of the holidays."

"What? Are you kidding me?"

"Hear me out," he interrupted. "We've got a supply barge coming in Monday, with lumber, flooring, and maybe the windows. We can get the house blocked in, tarp it up, and put everything on hold until after the first of the year."

"And we would do that why?"

"To live in harmony with mankind and the people who are just a football field away." Luke's chair creaked as he turned a little to look at Hunt. "It would be the right thing."

"Right thing? What I'm doing is the damn right thing...for me." He extended his legs in front of him and looked up at the lavender and rose sky. "Luke. I know what I need. Maybe that makes me a selfish ass, but I'm trying to make a home here. Set down some kind of roots and continuity. It's long overdue."

"I hear you." Luke sighed. "Without us stopping construction and cleaning up and securing the site, it's too dangerous to have people walking around out here. Especially at night." Luke opened a bag of potato chips that Hunt hadn't seen him bring out and shook the bag toward him. Hunt took a handful. "Alligators don't like mesquite potato chips, do they?"

Hunt laughed as he saw a six-foot gator swim past into the glow of the Christmas lights reflecting on the bayou. A fish, then another and another skipped out of the water, leaping at the brightest of the spots on the water created by the animated, lighted Santa in a pirogue being pulled by three gators. The first one had a red nose.

"I'm going to get our fishing poles. We've just been given a nice perk with those lights – attracting fish." Luke leaped from his chair. "We'll eat fried fish instead of bologna sandwiches tonight."

Forty-five minutes later, the parade of boats was heading back to Fa La La. Hunt spotted their cheerful lights and heard the singing of "Jingle Bells." Sound and light carried far on the water. He reeled in his line and picked up his camera.

"Man, that's pretty," Luke said, placing the bragging-rights redfish he caught into a second ice chest that also held two speckled trout.

Hunt didn't answer Luke. He was moving, adjusting his angle and aperture to capture the bright, crescent moon, hanging low over the glittering oyster boats, shrimp boats, and smaller recreational fishing boats. The way the reflected lights on the water streaked across the surface and the brighter lights of the boats above connected it all like holiday garland, it reminded him of a favorite Christmas train his parents had taken him to ride at the zoo when he was a small boy. The last time he'd ridden that train was when he was eleven. The year he got his first camera.

The year his parents died.

Chapter Five

The sunny kitchen at the back of her parents' small house smelled of freshly brewed coffee and the buttermilk biscuits rising in the oven. Camille loved this room. She was glad it remained exactly as it was when she was a little girl, except for the new stainless steel refrigerator. There were the same warm oak cabinets, white lace curtains, and marble-patterned Formica countertops that made the kitchen feel homey and comfortable.

Camille took her Christmas coffee mug, filled with dark, strong coffee, to the stove to add boiled milk to it. "I don't know why I don't boil milk when I make my coffee before work," she told her parents, who were reading the *Cane Gazette* at the old round oak table.

Her momma placed the section of the newspaper she was reading on the table. Her papa kept right on reading. "If I know my daughter, and I do," she said with a smile as bright as her candy-apple red sweat suit with its pistachio-green rickrack trim, "it's because you've slept to the very last moment and you don't have the time to do it."

"True." She inhaled deeply, enjoying the creamy and sweet rich scent. "It smells like marshmallows do when they're softened over an open flame."

"Not here for Christmas this year," June said, sounding sad. "Last night, there were so many people who asked why we didn't have the marshmallows roast, live reindeer, bonfire, and lover's path to the mistletoe gazebo, like before."

"Yeah, I know." She'd simply told them that they were working on it...and she intended to do just that, although she wasn't sure how. She sat across from her momma, who was now fingering the corner of the newspaper in front of her.

"Hunt has rejected every single attempt our family has made to get him to change his mind. We're all hoping you could make him have a change of heart." She smiled and stared into Camille's eyes, indicating that what she said had more than one meaning. What was her mother trying to tell her? "The heart is a peculiar thing. You never know when it can flip or soften..."

"Or harden," her papa said from behind his paper. "Hunt not letting us on da island has nothing to do wit his heart."

"Oh, sure it does," June said looking at her husband, daring him to disagree. He huffed and rattled his newspaper, but didn't say anything more.

"He's stubborn," Camille said. "Does that come from the heart?"

"It could."

"Heart." Her papa grumbled. "Youz make us losing half our revenue for da year sound romantic. Nothing romantic about us having to get a second and third job at our age. And that's if anyone would want to hire sixty-three-year-olds."

June shook her head and lifted her paper. "Camille will save us. You'll see." She started reading again.

Dear Lord. Momma and the people of Fa La La expect a miracle – and they expect me to be the miracle maker. Her stomach pinched. She wanted to do it for her family, friends, the visitors who came to the Christmas celebration. She had no idea how. Camille thought about the immovable Hunter James. If his actions hadn't told her just how stubborn he was, the set of his strong jaw and knowing eyes would've. His smooth good looks would've told her how sexy he was too. He had to be one of the most strong-willed men she'd ever met, and the sexiest.

Holy Cow. Why am I thinking of that?

Edward walked into the kitchen, dark circles under his tired eyes. He greeted everyone, but went straight to the coffeemaker on the counter. He was dressed for the day in well-fitted black jeans and another long-sleeved Christmas shirt one of her cousins had lent him. This one was pea-green with an extremely big-eared elf hand-painted on the front. It made her chuckle seeing him in it and she snapped a photo of him with her phone.

"Delete that," he said, his voice devoid of humor. "If you don't, I'll take a picture of you wearing those silly white shrimp boots." Her folks dropped their papers, looking at Camille with narrowed, disapproving eyes. She saw in their tight features that they couldn't believe she'd brought an arrogant man like this home to them. She should defend him, she knew, but she didn't want to. He wasn't an arrogant man, just uninformed and unaccustomed to their ways. Had she been that way with their co-workers in New York?

Camille liked to think she hadn't been. She didn't remember feeling or seeing negative reactions from those around her because she'd said things to insult others while she was there. She'd been away from Fa La La during college, residency and on a medical ship where she was exposed to a variety of lifestyles different then her own. It had been hard to adjust to and understand, but it was also fascinating to do so. Still, maybe she had inadvertently hurt others as Edward was doing now. She understood there was no malice in Edward's words, but he'd insulted her family nonetheless...again and again. And that upset her too.

Was she being fair to a good friend by empathizing with her family more than him? What was going on here was more than just this, she realized.

She got up and went to where he was struggling to lift the coffeepot with his swollen bee-stung hand. "Ix-nay on the shrimp boots." She poured him a mug of the strong, dark coffee that he liked to drink black. "Let's go outside to have our coffee." She walked away without waiting for him to answer.

Camille knew she was about to hurt him and that bothered her. She was a physician who healed, not wounded. She settled on the glider swing facing the bayou. The call of a blue heron, the croak of a frog, and the distant hammering on Hunt's new house carried on the slight breeze. She ignored them as she cleared her head to focus on what she had to communicate to Edward.

He sat next to her, his leg touching hers. "I'm glad to have this time alone," he said, his voice soft, relaxed. "We haven't had a moment to ourselves since we got here. I'm getting kind of lost with all the Christmas stuff and with your overwhelming family...As charming as they are, they're always around."

"This is their home, Edward. Of course, they're always around." He looked at her, his eyes telling her that he was surprised by her reply. She knew it was because while they were in New York, she'd told him that her family was always in her personal space. Hearing him say it, made her feel defensive, though. "I understand that Fa La La is completely different from where you grew up and where you work today. It takes open-mindedness and humility to appreciate that. While I think you are trying to get along and be friendly with my family and friends, I think you really don't understand them or want to."

"That's ridiculous," He tugged on the hem of his T-shirt. "Look at the butt-ugly shirt I'm wearing, Camille. I think that shows a hell of lot of humility and open-mindedness. It's a Christmas shirt. I'm Jewish."

She smiled and patted his hand. "I never would've thought I'd see you in these kinds of t-shirts." She sighed. "But, be honest. You're wearing them to keep from getting eaten alive by the mosquitoes." He exhaled hard and looked away. "Edward, I think you've been tolerant, not open-minded." She put her mug on the ground. "I say that because of the unguarded comments you've made that have hurt my family. Just now, you threatened to take a photo of me in *silly shrimp boots,* as if it was a bad thing and something that would embarrass me if our mutual friends saw it. And you said that in front of my parents, who work in those shrimp boots on a daily basis."

He looked at her. "What I..." He closed his mouth and didn't finish what he was about to say. He stared at her, realizing instantly that it was indefensible.

"There were other comments and facial expressions that weren't intentionally cruel, but telling nonetheless." She sighed, again. "Look. I get it. But I don't like it."

"Give me time," He reached for her hands. She didn't pull away. "Don't you know I'll do anything for you...because I love you. We're good together."

Part of Camille understood he was a good man and would come to appreciate and care about her family. Another part, the part that kept her heart sound and whole now, told her it didn't matter that he was a good man because he wasn't *her* man. He didn't make her feel tingly when she held his hand or when she kissed him good night before they went to their separate bedrooms. Not that she was in love with Hunt by any stretch of the imagination, but the way he'd made her feel when he simply took her hand to cross a stream on his island, and when he kissed her so briefly, after they argued on Thanksgiving day—the sparks were undeniable. There was an instant and strong sexual chemistry between them that she didn't have with Edward. While she wouldn't act on the chemical and biological attraction with Hunt, she wondered why she didn't have it with Edward, and why she hadn't been pleased to know his feelings for her ran so deeply.

She pulled her hands from him. "Edward, I'm not in love with you." He closed his eyes, but didn't move. "I'm sorry. I care about you. I think you're capable of..."

"Don't give me that 'it's not you, it's me' spiel. You're better than that." He opened his eyes and turned to face her. "How long have you known?"

"That you loved me or that I didn't love you?"

He looked up at the bright, cloudless blue sky. "Both."

"Yesterday, when I was treating your bee sting," she said honestly. "I saw in your eyes how deep your feelings were for me." She looked out over the bayou where a driftwood log floated by on the lazy current.

He stood, walked to the railing and rested his arms on it. "I feel like an idiot."

She went to him and rested her head on his shoulder. "I can't tell you how to feel, but I can tell you that you have no reason to feel that way. We did have a relationship that was going somewhere. It's just that when I came home, I got, oh, I don't know, more centered, I suppose." She could tell him that his offhanded comments had pushed her to see this, but she couldn't now, seeing his hurt. "I was lost and lonely in the city, Edward. I felt so out of place there, like you feel here in the bayou. You were kind to me and helped me get through some difficult days. I can't do that for you here, because you know you're leaving soon. I thought I was staying in New York. That's a big difference."

He nodded. "Yeah. I don't ever plan to live here."

"Me either. But my heart is still from here and beats as if I do live here." She shrugged. "I think that vulnerable woman you met is who you fell in love with. Not this woman who really, really loves being with her family. Who misses that brown bayou and the moss in the trees hanging over it." She smiled. "And the white shrimp boots you think are silly looking."

He laughed softly. "Yeah. I guess I was worried you would. That's why I wanted to come here with you, to remind you what you had in New York."

"You did exactly that, but didn't get the results you hoped for."

He held up his bee-stung hand and pointed to his mosquito-bitten face. "Louisiana told me to leave. It wanted you for itself."

"You just got stung by bees and bitten by mosquitoes. Don't read something conspiratorial into it." She kissed him on the cheek.

"That's interesting. I wonder if you've been doing that with how your family presses their opinions and will on you." He exhaled, sounding defeated.

Was Edward right? Had she misread her family as conspiratorial all of these years, misjudging the way they imposed their hopes and views on her? Had she just looked at the situation incorrectly? Or was she doubting what she'd come to believe because she'd fallen in love with her family again? "Maybe you're right," she conceded. His head came up, his eyes came to her, looking like he hoped she'd changed her mind about him. "About my family, I mean. I'm sorry," she sighed. "You're a dear..."

"Please don't tell me you like me as a friend. I'm not ready to hear that." He took a step away from her. "And Camille, don't tell me that you don't want me because you've fallen for Hunt."

"What? No. Of course not." In love with Hunt? Where in the hell did that come from? That was ridiculous.

He nodded, not looking convinced. "It's time for me to go home."

Edward went inside, packed, reschedule his travel arrangements, and got a ride to the boat dock, where the cab he'd called, was waiting to take him to the airport. He wouldn't let her or anyone else from the family drive him.

She sat at the kitchen table with her momma and papa, who didn't ask her why Edward had left so abruptly. They knew. They'd been expecting it. The screen door creaked open and her younger brother, René, charged into the kitchen with his usual vigor. Her mother had always said he was born with the darkest hair, the loudest cry, and the hardest kick. He was the sibling that had the biggest personality, although he was the smallest of the men at five-foot-six.

His kissed their momma on the cheek and then Camille. "I heard your doctor left," he said, reaching for one of the plump, flaky, and golden homemade biscuits in a pan on the stove. He carried it to the table and took a bite. It smelled like warm, buttery love and her youth. "You sure know how to make the Fa La La gossip flow."

"A talent I wish I didn't have." She shook her head. "Edward's gone. We weren't right for each other. That's all I'm saying on the subject, so don't ask anymore."

"That pretty much sums up what I've already heard," René said, his mouth full.

Her papa stood, carrying his empty coffee mug, but stopped behind her and kissed her with a long, hard press of his lips and thick beard on the cheek. Her heart broke a little. That was how he'd kissed her good-bye the day she'd left Fa La La, not knowing if she'd ever return. And also knowing that he was part of the reason she was leaving. Was he thinking of that now? He went to the coffeepot and poured another mug of coffee.

"Hey Papa," René said, around a mouthful of biscuit. "Remember that thunk I thought I heard when I pushed the starter on my boat?" T-Dud grunted. "Well, you were right. It was more of a clunk."

"I tole you it was probably a clunk. You need to know da difference wit youz thunks and clunks. So it was a bad solenoid, huh?"

"Yes, sir. I replaced the solenoid and she sounds like a well-loved woman."

"René!" their mother shouted, disapproving his analogy.

He laughed and winked at Camille. "Want to come with me to talk to the Scrooge since you know him best?" he asked. "I want to see if he'll let me take some mistletoe from his trees. I took my boat out this morning looking for some elsewhere, but I didn't see any. To save time and money, we should ask Scrooge."

"What are you going to do with the mistletoe?" June asked.

"I'm going to make a mistletoe arch on the back walkway near Tante Pearl's house," René took Camille's coffee mug and drank from it.

"Hey, that's mine," she complained, taking it back.

"Back there, it's sort of secluded and might appease the people who are disappointed that they cain't go to the mistletoe gazebo on the island."

T-Dud put his newspaper down. "Have youz spoken to Tante Pearl about dis? She'z likely to chase lovers away wit her broom. She won't like frisky couples near her house."

"I did talk to her. And she agreed to it when I told her she could set up a table nearby and sell her homemade broken glass and stained glass candy. She can make it peppermint flavored so our guests can have fresh breath when they lock lips." He laughed, tucking his clean white T-shirt into his faded Wranglers. "It ain't going to be the same as taking a long walk to get your kiss at the end under the gazebo, though."

"I'll go with you," Camille stood. "I have another idea that might get him to let us use the island." Besides, she needed to get away from Fa La La and clear her head.

***

"Are you afraid to be alone with me, Camille?" Hunt murmured as he watched Camille and her brother René, whom he'd met the day before at Fa La La, walk down his wharf and up the rise toward him on the front porch of his cabin. He rose out of his rocker and walked down the porch steps.

Camille didn't look like a woman who set broken bones and stitched gaping wounds, in her dark green, thigh-skimming shorts and red-and-white flannel shirt. With each step she took in her chunky white shrimp boots, her muscles bunched and elongated along her well-formed legs.

"Hello," René shouted when they were about twelve feet away. He was in his late twenties, but his baritone voice could've belonged to a man in his forties. It carried easily over the distant sounds of hammering and sawing from where workers were building Hunt's home acres away. "Beautiful morning, isn't it?"

Hunt nodded, looking at Camille, who wore the warm morning sunlight on her hair, face, and exposed legs like it was liquid gold. He'd taken a photo once that captured the sun as perfectly as she did now. He'd used the spot meter mode, bounced the light with a reflector, and exposed only the young Ute Indian woman as she performed a Sun Dance across the top of a still sand dune in the Great Sand Dunes National Park. The result was magic and a cover of *National Geographic,* and had also won him the coveted Pulitzer Prize for photography that year.

"Good morning, Hunt," Camille said, lifting her hand over her brow to block out the sun to look at him. Didn't she ever wear sunglasses?

"Good morning. Have you come for the Thanksgiving photos?" He'd meant to tell her before he'd left that he'd e-mail them to her or put them on a thumb drive and drop it off at the mercantile, but he'd forgotten when all he could think about was kissing her tempting mouth. Off limits, he reminded himself, thinking about Edward who was probably resting somewhere with calamine lotion on his body.

"We're actually here for mistletoe," René looked up into the trees around them. "We're hoping since you won't let us have our mistletoe gazebo here on your island, you'll agree to let us harvest some to use at Fa La La. You have the best mistletoe for miles around."

"Mistletoe?" Hunt didn't know what mistletoe actually looked like unless it had a bow wrapped around it and hung over a doorway.

"Actually, I'd love to get a copy of those photos." Camille smiled. "But René is right. We're here to ask you if we can have some of your mistletoe. I don't see any in these trees here," she said, tucking her hands in her pockets. "But you have a good bit on the back side of the island."

"Oh, you mean at my construction site?"

René huffed and Camille touched his arm in a silent gesture to calm down. Hunt appreciated that her temper wasn't as volatile as those of the men in her family.

"We'll sign a release of liability if you want. The mistletoe is almost as important to us as the use of your island." She looked at him, waiting for him to respond.

"Can't you just buy the ones I saw in the tiny plastic bags at the check-out counter at the Piggly Wiggly?" Both Camille and René made sounds of shock and distaste. He held up his hands. "Okay. Okay. That bad, huh?"

"Yeah, that bad. It'd be like you taking photos with a disposable cardboard camera," she countered. He laughed and saw her eyes soften. It sent a huge wave of heat through his body.

"I'm not agreeing; I just want to see where this mistletoe is that you want. We'll go from there."

René extended his hand. "Deal." Hunt shook it.

The three of them walked toward where he was building his house. The sounds of construction grew louder as they got closer to it. When they reached the small stream and thick marsh grass around it, he extended his hand to Camille. She smiled and pointed to her shrimp boots. "I've got these, thank you."

He felt disappointed, as ridiculous as it was. He'd been thinking about holding her hand at this stream since they'd started walking. No harm with that even if with her boyfriend around.

"There." Camille pointed to a tall cypress tree right alongside where his house was being constructed. "And there in the oak tree, and there." She pointed to two other trees in the same area with a heavy understory of palmetto.

"Where, in those trees?"

"Those wide, dark green clumps surrounding the branches in the trees are mistletoe," René said. "You really have a lot of it; some of those clumps look like they're five feet across. It's in those trees over there too."

Hunter hadn't really paid much attention to the darker patches of green in the trees before. Maybe he should just give it to them. "What is mistletoe anyway? Will it hurt the tree if you remove some of it? And how will you remove it?"

René started to answer, but Camille touched his arm again. Hunter wanted her to touch his arm instead. It was insane. René picked up a stick, walked about ten feet away from them and started nudging a frog that had hopped in front of him. Then he took a few steps farther away and looked up at the house. "While you two hash this out, do you mind if I take a look at your new house, Hunt? One of my buddies is your carpenter and while he hasn't given me any specifics, he's taken a lot of pride in what he's doing here. I'd like to see it for myself."

Hunt shrugged. Why not? It would give him some time alone with Camille. "Sure."

"Great." René winked at Camille and took off toward the construction site.

"To answer your question on how we will harvest the mistletoe," she said, picking up the conversation. "We'll use a bucket lift. One of our family members has one. It'll make it easy to get to the mistletoe. And to answer your other question, removing it is good for the tree. That's because it's actually a parasite spread into the trees by bird droppings." Hunter turned to face her.

"And that inspires kissing how...?"

She laughed. "Tradition. That's how, Hunter." She smiled, happy to have made her tradition point, yet again. "Mistletoe has a long history. The ancient Druids thought it was sacred and was a symbol of hope and fertility because it could bloom in the frozen winters. In Norse mythology, the goddess of love declared mistletoe a symbol of love and vowed to kiss all who passed beneath it. The Greeks once considered it a symbol of fertility and used it in primitive marriage rites. In England in the middle ages, men were allowed to steal a kiss from any woman caught standing under the mistletoe and the Kissing Bough. Refusing was considered bad luck." She laughed. "There's more traditions around the world with mistletoe, if you want to hear it."

Hunt wondered if she would kiss him if he brought her to stand under the mistletoe right now. Because of all she claimed about believing in tradition, he suspected she would without a second thought of Calamine covered Edward.

"Our tradition for Fa La La," she continued, "is to use the Kissing Bough with the mistletoe to create a huge centerpiece in the gazebo."

"And the Kissing Bough is what?"

"It's a round decoration that's traditionally decorated with nuts, fruits, greenery, and herbs...and mistletoe for the communities that don't find it too naughty and pagan. We've made them with things we find around Fa La La, including mistletoe from your island."

"So you don't find it too naughty, then?" He took a step closer to her. She didn't look away. He saw a bit of mischief and promise in her eyes.

"Not at all. I think it's fun."

Now he was standing within six inches of her. Her breathing was heavier, and so was his. He lowered his voice. "Do you let Edward kiss you under the mistletoe?"

"Not anymore," she whispered. "Not that we were ever really a couple, but he's gone."

"Well, then, I intend to kiss you under the mistletoe and other places too, Doc."

Camille looked at his mouth and he nearly pulled her against him to kiss her then and there, mistletoe or Kissing Bough be damned. The bright blue sky and white puffy clouds would work just fine. But the hammering suddenly stopped and the ensuing silence was like a huge bucket of ice water being thrown in his face.

She swallowed hard. "I guess René made his entrance."

"Guess so." He took her hand. It felt warm and comfortable, like a blazing fire on a chilly day. "Let's get those Thanksgiving photos and talk about harvesting the mistletoe."

"So we *can* harvest it?" She didn't pull her hand away and he liked that, a lot.

"Yes. Under my conditions." He led her toward the cabin. "Now, tell me more about the Kissing Bough and the kissing tradition."

Chapter Six

"My darkroom's inside," Hunt said when they reached the lopsided porch to his cabin. He released her hand and stepped forward.

Camille hesitated a moment, thinking she should tell him she'd wait on the porch for him to bring the thumb drive to her. That was absurd. She was much too old to play the fearful virgin, protecting her reputation. That wasn't a role she'd ever played. Besides, Hunt wouldn't jump her unless she indicated she wanted him to. He'd said they would talk about the harvesting of the mistletoe. That was progress. She smiled. He was finally agreeing to something they'd requested. Maybe he'd be agreeable to the other thing she wanted to present to him.

She slipped off her shrimp boots, as he had his shoes, both walking into the cabin in their socks – hers, red-and-white stripes with leaping reindeer; his, simple black athletic socks. Inside, she was immediately struck by the cool, air-conditioned temperature. Once her eyes adjusted to the dim light, she saw that she'd been right about him not remodeling the cabin. The pine paneling and terra-cotta linoleum was just as she remembered. The plywood, doorless cabinets were the same ones Mr. Gaudet had installed years ago. There was a new refrigerator, a microwave, and a one-cup-at-a-time coffeemaker. In the space used for a living room, there were two new, moss-gray leather recliners and a deep moss-gray leather sofa. A huge, man-dream-sized TV covered almost the entire width of a wall, blocking a window behind it.

"That's totally over-the-top," she laughed, pointing to the television.

"I need it for work."

"What, are you a microbiologist studying the epidermis of football and basketball players?" She didn't wait for him to respond; something came to her from what he'd said earlier. "You said darkroom."

He smiled and sat in one of the recliners. "Have a seat." She sat on the other recliner. The leather was smooth and cold against the back of her legs.

"Brr. It's cold in here." She wrapped her arms around her waist.

"I'll share my body heat." His dark eyes were a bit playful.

"You're such a flirt." She laughed. "And I know flirts. I've had more little old men patients that are as frisky as you than I can count."

"I'm neither little nor old," he pointed out. "When you walk into their treatment room, I bet they think they've died and gone to heaven."

She laughed again. "Most are so darling." She spotted his camera on the kitchen table, reminding her what she wanted to talk to him about. "Change of subject." She shifted to sit on the edge of the recliner. She would get him saying yes, then ask the question that she thought might get him to agree to allow the Christmas Celebration back onto Cypress Island. "I'm glad you joined us for Thanksgiving yesterday. Did you enjoy yourself?"

"The food was amazing. Your mother and everyone who prepared the meal are incredible cooks. Luke chastised me for not bringing home leftovers, though. It was good enough to serve at any five-star Michelin restaurant. You made the potato salad, right?"

She smiled. "I don't cook, but I'm a great assembler of ingredients." She smiled. "I'll bring y'all some. I'm sorry I didn't think about it yesterday." Of course, he had totally befuddled her with his warm looks and sensual kiss. "Thank you for agreeing to let us harvest some mistletoe. We will be very respectful of your property. May we come tomorrow?"

He shrugged. "Yeah. That's fine."

Okay, she gotten two yeses. He seemed relaxed and agreeable. "You're really a good photographer. An enthusiastic one too."

His eyes were so intelligent and soul-searching, she had to look away. She worried he would see right through her and know what she was trying to do before she did it. She needed to ease him into it, if she was to have any chance of succeeding.

"It's pretty exciting that you get paid for doing what you love. Can you imagine if you could do what you love, get paid for it, and stay here on your beloved island?"

"Yes. That thought has crossed my mind."

Good. She was still heading in the right direction. She was getting positive responses. "I have an idea that you might like, then." She rested her elbows on her knees. "What do you think about being the official photographer of the Fa La La *Cajun Christmas on the Bayou Celebration*?"

He bit his bottom lip, but didn't outright turn her down.

"This is what I propose. We can create a really nice backdrop, keeping with the Cajun theme, and you can take photos of people standing in front of it." She looked at him and couldn't tell from his expression what he was thinking. "Think of all the memories you would capture for so many families. You'd get to do what you like, make people happy, and make a lot of money, all at the same time. You can charge whatever you want, Hunter. We'll advertise it for you with signage posting the details and prices you set."

"That's an interesting proposal, Camille." He rubbed his chin and she held her breath. He was giving it a fair consideration. "Maybe, if this goes well, I might get enough gigs locally to pay my bills so I never have to travel away from my island." Yes. Oh, it was going to work. This idea was going to be a win-win for him and Fa La La. She pinched her hand to keep from showing too much excitement. She couldn't do that until she got him to agree.

"I think people would want to hire you for their weddings, anniversary celebrations, and other events. The women of Cane would absolutely love spending time with a handsome man like you."

"You think I'm handsome, huh?"

"Yes. I ..." She smiled at him. "You are really roguish, Hunter James." Now she needed to go for the close. "What do you say? Let's do this. You become the official photographer for Cajun Bayou Christmas, we set up a beautiful backdrop on Cypress Island so you can take the photos, and we create traffic for you by having our bonfire, live reindeer, and mistletoe gazebo. Is that a yes?"

"I can charge my hourly rate, huh?" She nodded. "Weddings and anniversary parties, huh?" She nodded again. He stood, extended his hand to her. She accepted it and stood when he tugged for her to do so. "Let's see if you like my work first."

When he turned his back to her, she squeezed her eyes shut and pumped her fist. This was going to work. Fa La La would earn enough money to sustain their way of life another year. He opened the door to the right of the living room and flicked on a light. Hanging on two thin lines from one wall to another on the right side were a dozen photos clipped to them with wooden clothespins. On the left side of the room was a queen-sized bed, covered with a white down comforter and three fluffy pillows. Under the lines was a desk, with a large monitor on top of it.

"Your darkroom is your bedroom too?"

He looked at her and smiled. "Yes."

Her cell phone pinged with a text. Habit from being on call had her reaching for it. "It's René. He says it's raining." She listened a moment, then pointed up when she heard the rain hitting the tin roof. "He's helping hang tarps to secure your house. Then Luke's taking them all to lunch at the café in Cane before he goes to the lumberyard." She looked at Hunt. "He asked if I can get a ride back to Fa La La with you. Can I?"

"Of course," he said, having to speak louder now that the rain was really pounding on the tin roof. He sat in the squeaky wooden chair and turned on his computer as she texted her reply.

"You have both old-school and modern photo processing, I see." She pointed to where his sophisticated printer was sitting on the table next to the chemical trays, tongs, and enlarger.

"I keep my developer, stop bath, and fixer outside of this tinderbox cabin. I fill the pans in the shed out back and carry them in here when I need them."

"Good idea." She walked to look at the photos on the lines. The first was of a small, dark-complexioned boy, wearing a dusty turban and tattered clothes, sitting astride a small elephant, with a man who was dressed similarly sitting aside a much larger elephant beside him. There was something so compelling about the photos that went beyond the beauty of the composition. It told a story about these men – father and son. The next photo was of a woman, sitting cross-legged in a market. Like the boy and his father on the elephants, the focus was on her face, her life. Tears sprang to Camille's eyes seeing the sadness in the woman's eyes as she smiled with broken front teeth, looking at the camera. Her hands, busy braiding colorful yarns, were missing two fingers.

"India?" she asked, wiping her tears. He nodded, looking at her. "These are incredible. The emotion you captured with the light in their eyes and the shadows on their faces is remarkable." She turned to look at him. "You aren't just a photographer that works where you're paid to work, are you?"

"That's what I do. Mostly." He picked up a magazine off his desk and handed it to her.

"You did this." She didn't ask; she knew. She'd only looked at two photographs he'd taken and she saw the same point of view in those as she did in this one of an Indian woman dancing on a bright cream-colored sand dune. Her face held both joy and a history of tragedy. "Who are you?"

"Just a guy who wants some peace." She moved to stand closer to him. She was drawn to him in such a fire of emotions, wanting to understand this man who saw so much in the faces of others. Of course he'd want peace, and the fact that this was how he answered her was telling.

"It must take a lot out of you to feel and empathize and know the people you capture. To touch a soul is to be consumed by it."

He sucked in a breath as if she had placed a hot branding iron against his heart. He took a step back. She took a step forward. She placed her hand on his chest.

"Can this island really give you the peace you seek? Can it come from a place?"

"I don't know." She knew he answered with honesty. "I've got to try. I've seen a lot of hatred, death in war and in poverty and in wealth. I've crawled on my belly right beside someone who was wondering if he would survive the battle and who died a second later." He ran his hand down the full length of her hair. "I don't know if I can ever feel peace, Camille. But I've got to try before what I do consumes me."

She rested her head on his chest and wrapped her arms around him. She had no words for him. She just wanted him to feel comfort and support with no strings attached. He didn't put his arms around her for a long thirty seconds. Then, he gathered her hair into his hand and pulled her harder against his chest. And exhaled.

They just stood there, holding one another under the brightness of the old ceiling fixture, on the cut linoleum floor, with the treasures of his photography around them. Camille knew in that instant, she could not and would not ask him to share his island with her family and the strangers they would bring there. No matter how much she knew they were counting on her to save their way of life, she couldn't do it. She would disappoint them again and fail them when they needed her most. Good thing she was leaving soon or she too would be consumed by the people she loved. She shivered.

"Cold?" he asked, his voice so deep it touched somewhere deep inside of her. He turned, fitting her shorter body against his. She felt his warm breath on her hair.

"Not at all. I feel feverish." She licked her lips, because her mouth was so dry from nerves and sudden desire.

"Are you feeling hot, Camille?" His grin was dark, sexy, and a bit mischievous. She nodded, resting her hands on his shoulders. "Me too." He touched his lips to hers, gently tasting her bottom lip, the corners of her mouth. She squeezed his shoulders, needing to hold on, because her knees suddenly felt weak. His hands tightened on her hips, she felt his fierce desire in each fingertip digging in her flesh and in the firmness of his body.

"Please kiss me, Hunt. Kiss me." He did. Angling his head, he pressed his soft, wet mouth against hers, his tongue finding hers, tender one moment, anxious and needy the next. It flared into each nerve ending in her body as blood raced hot and fast through her.

Hunt's hands moved from her hips to beneath her thighs as he lifted her into his arms and carried her to his bed. He never stopped kissing her, on her mouth and along the sensitive area along her jawline and ears. The mattress dipped beneath their weight as he lowered her onto the cool, cotton duvet filled with soft down. It had his clean, musky scent and that gave her pleasure too, knowing she was wrapped in the wonderful scent of this beautiful man.

He kneeled, looking down at her, his face shadowed with the ceiling light shining behind him. She couldn't see his eyes, but she felt the intensity of them on her. She smiled and saw his shoulders rise, when he took a deep breath. He pulled off his shirt, and she saw his muscles rippling on his abdomen as his arms lifted over his head and blocked out the bright light for a moment. She reached up, her sensitive fingertips trained to feel and examine without seeing. She felt the tight ridges of hard muscle over bone not as a, physician but as a woman who desired a man in a way she'd never desired anyone before.

Hunt covered her hand with his, and guided it to his hard flat nipples. She sat up, then knelt with him, her mouth and tongue exploring the small nub, enjoying the feel and taste of this gorgeous man. His fingers dug into her hips and pulled her against his hard center.

"You're killing me," he groaned, pushing her back onto the mattress and following her down, careful to not let his weight crush her. His movements were less controlled and clumsier now. He nearly ripped the buttons off of her shirt as he tried to undress her with trembling fingers. When he reached for the buttons of her shorts, he cursed. "How many damn buttons do you have?" She laughed, and gave him a gentle push until she was on top.

"I've got this." She got up, stood next to the bed and looked at him. His face was no longer in the shadows, but spotlighted like he was center stage on Broadway. He propped a pillow behind his head, the top button of his jeans undone, one leg bent to the side, the other straight in front of him. When she was back in New York after a long shift, in those lonely minutes before she fell asleep, this image of Hunt was what she'd think of. She already knew she'd remember this incredible experience with him, and they weren't close to being finished. She hoped he'd think of her too. She would make sure he did. Somehow it seemed important that he did.

She looked at his eyes, burning with desire as he watched her undress for him. She took her time, when all she wanted to do was hurry back into his hot embrace. She pinched the tab of the zipper and slowly lowered it, hearing each metal tooth opening in a sensual tune, promising him that soon what lay beneath would be theirs to share. His hand settled over his heart. Was it beating as wildly as hers?

Camille hooked her thumbs in the waistband and slowly swayed her hips back and forth as she lowered her shorts, until they were at her knees. She let them drop to the floor and he sucked in a hard breath. Perspiration trickled down the center of his chest.

He reached for her, but she shook her head, running her hands over her deep red Christmas lace bra until her fingers touched the candy cane clasp between her breasts. She let them pause there a moment. His hips shifted on the bed, his hand going to his zipper. It was his turn to tease her. He lowered it and let his jeans fall open in a promise of what was to come. She answered it with the click of her opening the bra. The sound filled the room, as did a deep guttural growl of appreciation and need that echoed up from his chest.

She pulled her bra off and let it drop to the floor.

"You are so beautiful," he said, the words caught on his heavy breath. She ran her finger slowly across the top of the green lace trimming her red silk panties. He nodded slowly, as she took her time, teasing him, moving her hips side to side as she eased them down her legs, until they rested at her ankles over her candy-cane-stripped socks. She kicked her panties aside. He tapped the bed beside him. "Leave the socks on," he said, his voice deep, sensual, with a hint of playfulness, like her socks. He tapped the bed again. "Now, take off my clothes."

She smiled, enjoying this new and exciting foreplay. Heart pounding, her body aching for him to touch her as his eyes promised he would, she grabbed the sides of his jeans and pulled them down, letting her short nails scrape his long, muscled legs. No underwear. The man didn't wear underwear. She knew it would be something she'd think about later, like seeing him now so incredibly aroused and gorgeous. They were both naked now. She slid up his body, her breasts and nipples feeling the roughness of his hair and the smoothness of his skin. He lifted her to him until her mouth was even with his.

"I want you so bad, I hurt all over." His body quivered as his mouth crushed against hers and hers against his. He devoured her, like a man having his last meal, tasting and savoring along the column of her neck, over her collarbone, to the top of her full breasts and over her nipples. She wrapped her leg over his hip and felt the hard flex of his buttocks and thighs.

The heat and desire that had been building between them since they met boiled within them. Building. They trembled and felt the growing need pushing inside, until neither could wait any longer. He quickly reached into a backpack on the floor. Put on a condom, then flipped her onto her back, gently opened her legs, and entered her. Her world immediately exploded. He moved within her once more, threw his head back, and called out her name.

***

Hunt slept. His breathing was steady and strong against her chest, where his head rested, his arm heavy over her bare abdomen. She loved feeling the weight of him on her. She loved feeling him resting on her.

She simply loved him. But was she in love with him?

She'd been struck with a lightning bolt when she'd seen into his heart and soul through his photography. Before that, there had been chemistry, respect, and pleasure when they spent time together. His photos, though, were a window into the man.

She glanced toward those photos hanging on the lines. One, not very far away, caught her eye. She hadn't noticed it before. It was a photo of her. She quietly removed herself from under him and went to take a closer look. It was one of the ones he'd captured when she was playfully posing on the outside deck on Thanksgiving. There weren't any others from that day, she observed, wondering why. She peered at the photo, hoping for an answer. It was of her from the waist up, her arms extended, one up and one down. Her body was turned to the side, slightly, looking at Hunt over her shoulder. The breeze had picked up a few strands of her hair behind her, capturing movement.

"That's my favorite," he said, kissing her on the shoulder and drawing her back against his chest. "Your eyes are unguarded. Glowing with your inner spirit. The camera caught you in a single moment of happy abandonment."

"No. You did." She turned in his arms to face him. "You know what that photo makes me think of?"

"Making love to me?" He kissed her and she forgot what they were talking about until he reminded her a minute later. "What does it remind you of, Camille?"

"Happy milestones that signaled growth, change."

"What milestones?" He led her back to his bed, where they settled comfortably beneath the duvet.

"Taking the boat out by myself for the first time when I was eight. Learning to ride my bike on the walkways of Fa La La and then freaking out when I went to ride at a friend's on a regular street in her neighborhood. Getting my diploma from med school and seeing my papa's eyes and cheeks shiny with proud tears." She shifted onto her stomach and rested her arms on his chest and looked at him. "What milestones have you had, Hunt?"

He exhaled, tucking her hair behind her ear. She could see the one that came to mind for him was a sad one. "Going to live with my elderly grandparents when I was eleven. I barely knew them. They lived on a ranch in

Colorado. I had been living with my parents in Houston. It was a huge adjustment, not only because of the different landscape, lifestyle." He looked deeply into her eyes. "It was because I was so profoundly sad. My parents had died only two weeks before. I was alone. I felt completely alone and frightened."

Oh, God. Her heart broke for him. She'd never, ever had to live without knowing her parents were a plane, car, or boat ride away from her. "How did you survive that?" His eyes slowly settled on hers and she knew. "Your camera. You looked at the world through your camera, connecting to and distancing yourself from it. There was a barrier there between your emotions and life lived."

He nodded, paused a moment as his eyes grew dark and pensive. "I'm in awe of how you understand me."

"And I'm in awe of how you capture people in the world. It took your pain, your ability to adapt, to get you to that place." She slid up his body, until her face was even with his. "Not everyone adapts so well. What you have is a gift, Hunt. A gift born from what God handed you."

His hands slid along her back. "I wish I could give you what you want for your family and from them. I really do."

"I know."

"My parents gave me a camera for Christmas." He said it and she understood that he was gifting her with something so deep and intimate to him that he probably rarely shared it. "It was a week before they were killed by a drunk driver on their way to a New Year's Eve party. And, you should know, I don't hate Christmas because of that memory."

Camille kissed him. Their kisses were tender, slow, and so was their lovemaking. It was then that she knew she'd fallen in love with him.

Chapter Seven

Hunt woke up and felt the bed next to him, looking to pull Camille against him. He longed to feel her soft, amazingly beautiful naked body against his. She wasn't there.

He sat up and stretched his arms over his head. He picked up his phone from the nightstand. "Holy crap!" It was six a.m. He'd slept straight through to the next day. He felt wonderful. He was rested, satisfied, and he hadn't had any of the dreams that often haunted him.

Making love to Camille was only part of the reason he slept so soundly. A really great part. But it was their honest and open conversations that gave them true intimacy. The kind two people share when they're stripped bare of the obstacles that were created because they lack trust in the other person. For some reason, Hunt felt safe with Camille. He trusted her and exposed himself like he would the precious raw film from his camera that held images so easily destroyed, damaged or developed into something else. Maybe something wonderful.

As they lay naked together, touching and petting one another, they talked more about their childhoods, their dreams realized and lost. Through the trivial to the substantive, Hunt got to know Camille. She hated cherries but loved watermelon. Her favorite food was boiled crawfish. Her least favorite was canned tuna. She'd been skinny-dipping in the bayou when she was two and then again when she was seventeen. She said she wanted to go skinny-dipping with him when she turned thirty-five next month. With each discovery, Hunt liked her more and more and more. Now, he was missing her.

He stretched again, on a big yawn, and smiled. Clipped with one of his plain wooden clothespins on one of the photo lines next to the photo of her was a handwritten note for him. He got out of bed and laughed when he took the note from the line. It was true; doctors had awful penmanship.

Hunt,

I hope you had a long and peaceful sleep. I had to get back to Fa La. Luke's giving me a ride. I'd like to see you again, as my time here is growing short. I have to leave the day after tomorrow. Please join me for tomorrow's boat parade. If you slept through the night, that would actually be tonight—Saturday. Saturdays are special during the holidays for us, as we invite the public to join the procession. Meet at the docks at four.

Camille

P.S. I had a really wonderful time with you.

Hunt hung the note back on the line next to her photograph. He tapped his chest. It felt full and warm. Should he go and put himself on an inescapable boat with a group of people who didn't like him just so he could be with Camille? Or should he stay home, watch the parade from behind the lens of his camera? Either way, nothing could come of this powerful attraction between them. She was returning to New York on Monday. Her family and community would forever blame him for changing Christmas for them. Both weren't things that inspired relationships.

He walked into the bathroom and turned on the shower. What in the hell should he do?

***

Hunt turned off the engine to the outboard motor and let his small boat ease against the dock at Fa La La. It was cooler by about twenty degrees, since a cold front had come through as he and Camille had made love. The best night's sleep he'd had in months, he thought as the hull bumped the dock. Making love with Camille had been damn near perfect, except for the part where he'd woken alone. She should've still been in his arms. He'd anticipated making love with her slowly when they were both drowsy, and then starting their days.

The concept of having a woman there to wake up to was as odd for him as enjoying spending hours talking to her, albeit she was naked at the time. He'd never craved having his bed partner stay with him all night. Was it just an aberration or was it something else? He intended to find out. That's what drove him to put himself in the uncomfortable situation of riding in a boat parade with people trying to convince him to do something that would destroy the peace he'd only just figured out how to obtain.His friend Luke had come with him to give him some support and to make sure, in his words, "You don't make an ass of yourself."

Luke zipped the hooded sweatshirt that he wore over another sweatshirt and under his jean jacket. "It's damn chilly," he complained as he climbed out of the boat and secured the stern line, then caught the bow line that Hunt tossed to him.

"You can stay inside and watch *Dancing with the Stars* with the Fa La La elders if it's too cold for you out here." Hunt laughed, grabbed his camera bag, and joined his friend on the dock. The late afternoon sky reflected a bright coral glow and streaks of lavender on the rippling water.

"Do yourself a favor, Hunt, don't disappear behind that camera all night. Be part of the scene, not just an observer of it. You might be surprised what you see with your naked eyes rather than through the camera lens."

Before Hunt could respond, a full, thick Cajun-accented voice called from an approaching boat. "Catch my line, will you?" It came from a Lafitte skiff-style boat. Although the Christmas lights on the boat weren't lit yet, Hunt could see it was decorated with all red lights, except for a bright green buoy on the bow. It looked like it had a light inside of it.

"Happy to help," Hunt told him as he walked to the edge of the dock behind his boat to get the line from a man who looked as sturdy as an oak tree. He had two women on the boat with them. One appeared to be about his age, mid-fifties, the other much older. The older lady, in her late seventies or early eighties, was dressed like a bubblegum pink elf with knee-high white disco boots. Her silver-blue hair curled around her matching elf-cone hat that had a thick white pom-pom on the end. Hunt reached for the camera around his neck, realizing it wasn't there. She had a face that showed the wrinkles of a full life and a strong personality. He wanted to photograph her. He removed his camera from the bag, took off the lens cap, and turned it on.

"Do you mind if I take a photo of you?" Hunt showed her his camera.

"Of course not. Da camera loves me." She kicked out her go-go boot and smiled. He snapped a few photos and when she thought he was finished, he snapped more.

He helped Luke finish securing the lines, then extended his hand to help the elderly elf out of the boat. The fact that she was strong and sure-footed on blocky heels didn't surprise him.

"I know youz didn't ride youz motorcycle here," she told Hunt when she was on the dock. She rubbed the sleeve of his jacket. "Dat's good leather. Look at this, Ruby. I think we need to get us a motorcycle jacket," she told the red-haired woman wearing a bright green sweater dress that matched the buoy on the bow of the boat. Hunt extended his hand to help her onto the dock too. "Do youz think I can get it in pink?"

"That's real nice. It looks like a classic," she said, smiling at him. "I'm Ruby and that fashionista is my aunt, Tante Izzy." She waved to the man in the boat, standing in overalls with a green cone Santa hat hanging from his side pocket. "And that's my husband, Big John."

Big John got out of the boat and shook hands with Luke and Hunt. He was a giant of a man, his hands thick and beefy, and his happy-go-lucky personality sparkled in his eyes.

"I'm Hunt and this is Luke."

"Hunt? Da man who won't let us on da island?" Tante Izzy scowled. "Harrumph. I guess youz have reasons. I sure miss gettin' my kisses in da mistletoe gazebo." She looked up at him and narrowed her eyes. "Just so youz know, you may have a land title, but you don't own it."

"The state of Louisiana would disagree with you, Madame." What was she talking about?

"Youz don't own dat island, no more than you own da air and stars." She hooked her arm in the bend of his as Hunt helped her up the flight of stairs. He remembered Camille quoting Massasoit philosophy on the first day they met and grabbing at straws, looking for an excuse that would stick to get him to change his mind about using Cypress Island. From the tone of Tante Izzy's voice and the way her eyes narrowed, he knew she was being sincere.

"Youz have taken guardianship of it to make sure it is well cared for and gets to serve da purpose of why God put it there." She nodded. "And I think youz know da other part – it chose you."

"That's a perspective I hadn't considered." Hunt gently squeezed her frail hand.

"Well, youz think about it." As soon as they reached the walkway, Tante Izzy was enveloped by a group of ladies who were anxious to have her taste some cookies they'd baked for the night. Hunt changed the aperture and adjusted his focus for a shallow depth of field to capture them in a candid moment,

"Hunt." Camille rushed up to him, kissing him on the cheek. All his doubts about whether he should be there evaporated. Her wide, happy smile lit up her face as she stood with the late sun's tangerine and violet colors kissing her shoulders and black hair. She looked so beautiful in her jeans, red sweater, and short white jacket. Although he liked her best wearing nothing more than the candy-cane-striped socks she'd worn while they'd made love.

"You don't happen to have those red-and-white socks on inside those UGGs do you?"

She laughed. "Maybe you can find out later."

June, T-Dud, Mr. Dudley, Pierre, René and the rest of her siblings, nephews, and nieces told him hello and made their way down the stairs to their boats. Hell, when had he learned the names of so many people here?

"I'm glad you're here," Camille told him, touching his arm. "It's good you brought Luke too." She looked over her shoulder, where he was talking to René. "He'll ride with René. We'll ride on my papa's boat. It's the caboose in the parade, which I like best because we get to see all of the lighted boats in front of us. It's beautiful."

"Not dat it'z any of youz concern, but I didn't walk up by myself," Tante Izzy told Dudley. "Dat handsome Hunt escorted me." Camille laughed.

"Why, Hunt. I see you've got a fan."

"Yeah, I'm a pink elf magnet." He grabbed her hand. "Come with me." And she did.

They rushed past most of Fa La La's residents as they were heading toward the docks. He continued to walk at a brisk pace, turning right when he saw someone approaching from ahead of them and left, when someone approached from the right. Camille laughed, sounding young and happy as her boot-clad feet tried to keep up.

Finally, there were no more people around in the dark corner he randomly found at the back of Fa La La.

He spun her around, pushing her back against the wall of the building. He leaned into her, his leg moving between hers. He captured her mouth, like his very life depended on it, his tongue stroking hers in a soft, desperate, and sense-exploding kiss that had his hands trembling. He grabbed her butt and squeezed, remembering how her hot, naked flesh felt in his hands. Camille nipped his bottom lip, then gently stroked the spot with her tongue. When she blew on his wet, tender lips, he went blind.

"Light," she murmured when it flashed on. "Uh-oh." A second later, a little old lady wearing dark, cat's-eye glasses, yelling in Cajun French, started swatting them with a stiff-bristled broom. "Tante Pearl. Pardon. Pardon." She grabbed Hunt's hand. "Run." They ran like teenagers caught making out along the bayou side. He couldn't remember having laughed so hard in a very long time.

Soon, they all boarded the ten or so boats there, while other boats floating in the bayou, loaded with passengers, waited to join the parade. The scents of diesel fuel, the muddy bayou waters, and verdant marsh grass were carried on the light, northerly breeze, along with happy voices. There was such a palpable feeling of anticipation and pleasure around them. It surprised Hunt how much everyone seemed to enjoy the Fa La La Cajun Bayou Christmas Celebration, even though it was basically their job to be there. Of course, he'd always enjoyed his work.

The wheelhouse was well lit by fluorescent lights that hung on white marine paneled ceilings. It was well appointed with polished teak wood cabinets, counters and trim spanned the front of the cabin, with a narrow ledge along the walls. There were monitors, gages, and two laptops on the counter, along with levers and the boat's wooden helm. A queen-size bed on a platform with cabinets below it was to the rear of the cabin. He imagined there was another cabin or two below decks. He thought about having Camille taking him on a tour there, as a ruse to steal a kiss while they were away from the curious eyes of the people on board.

"Tante Pearl isn't on this boat, huh?" he asked with a grin.

Camille lifted a brow. "No. Why are you asking?" He lifted both his hands and smiled in response.

"What youz think, Hunt?" T-Dud motioned to the wheelhouse, where he looked comfortable captaining his boat. Hunt lifted the camera and snapped a photo of Captain T-Dud.

"She's a beauty," he said, then asked T-Dud about the type of engine he had on the boat and the equipment within his reach on the counter. T-Dud showed him the depth finders, GPS, radar, diagnostic and monitoring equipment, and temperature gages for the ice storage wells at the back of the boat. They discussed the functions of the boat and a little bit of its history. After about fifteen minutes, the radio crackled on a high shelf to his left. Hunt recognized Pierre's voice.

"We have sixteen boats tonight. Y'all know your positions in line. I'll move out first. Just follow after that."

Camille handed Hunt a cup of steaming hot chocolate. The white marshmallows started melting in a creamy puddle of richness on top of the thick, sweet drink. Their hands brushed for just a moment, and Camille's cheeks got pink. It pleased him more than it should have to see it.

"Take him outside for da boat parade," her father told her. She interlocked her fingers with Hunt's and led him to sit on a large ice chest below the high window of the wheelhouse, in the front of the boat. Here in the darkest shadows, no one could see them, unless they came to the bow of the boat.

Without preamble, the boat's lights went on, from bow to stern, from boom to boom, and along the edge of the wheelhouse. Various shades of blue, green, white, red, and gold lights illuminated the other boats and parts of Fa

La La too. It was a display of creativity, over exuberance, and style, as each boat had their own unique way of decorating. Some boats had extras like lighted *Joyeaux Noel* signs on both the port and starboard sides. Another had an animated blow-up snow globe with a Santa inside of it on top of their wheelhouse. And another had a lighted nativity with a Christmas Star suspended in the tall booms of their shrimp boat. While they all were decorated to the talents and tastes of the boat owners, the same music was shared by all. "Jingle Bell Rock" was playing now.

Camille sighed, looking out at the bayou. "There are as many lights shining on the water as there are stars in the sky tonight." She turned her head and looked up at Hunt. He bent down and kissed her tenderly. Sweet kisses under the glow of Christmas lights around them, on this cool, crisp evening felt as special and important as the hug she'd given him in his cabin that day. Both seemed to have rocked his world, touching a dark fearful place within him with Camille's special light. Both went beyond sexual desire, of which there was plenty. It was something...else.

She leaned to let her back rest on the front of the wheelhouse. Hunt did the same after he safely stowed his camera in its bag. Camille shivered and Hunt put his arm around her shoulder and pulled her against him to share his warmth. She relaxed against his chest. "I'm so glad you are here."

"It's a different perspective from onboard than from my island." He immediately thought about what Tante Izzy had said. It wasn't *his* island. He was guardian of it for future generations.

"It's a different perspective when you move away and return home for a visit too." The light breeze with the motion of the boat had their hair blowing away from their faces. "I'm going to miss it when I go back to work."

Hunt's heart felt like it stopped beating. "So you're going to return to New York?"

She nodded, scooted closer to him. "It's getting colder now that the sun is going down."

It felt colder to him knowing he wouldn't see her sunny smile. He knew he'd think of it every time he looked at Fa La La. "What's in New York that makes you want to go back there?"

"It's what's here that makes me want to go back to New York," she said, just as her mother walked up to them. Hunt knew she'd heard her daughter.

"I thought y'all would be cold," June said, handing them a large, heavy beige quilt stitched with a big sleigh overflowing with presents.

"Thank you," he said, unfolding the quilt and placing it over Camille's shoulders. "Would you like to join us?" Hunt saw the crushing hurt in June's eyes and thought maybe she needed some time to talk to her daughter. Although unintentionally, Camille's words had upset her mother.

"Thank you, Hunt, but I want to get the other quilts out for our guests." She walked away without making eye contact with her daughter.

"It's none of my business and you know how I feel about my privacy, so I'm going out of my comfort zone to tell you this." He pulled the quilt closed over her chest. "I've seen the way you've looked at your father with sadness in your eyes and I've seen the way your mother has looked at you with a sadness too. I don't know if what happened between you all, if anything has, is why you want to go back to New York, but your words just now, hurt your mother."

"What?" She sat up, the quilt falling off her shoulder. "I'd never say anything to hurt my mother..."

"You did." He picked up the quilt and put it on her again.

She shoved his hands away and adjusted the quilt herself. "Tell me what you're talking about."

"*It's what's here that makes me want to go back to New York.*" He lifted her chin when she looked down at her knees. "June heard you."

Tears filled her eyes. "I'm so awful." He brushed away the tears. "I chastised Edward for doing the same thing. Saying hurtful things about my family in ways that were not meant to be insulting but derogatory nonetheless. And I've been upset by unpleasant things that were said about me when the person saying it didn't know I had heard him. Now, I'm doing the same thing."

"Are all of those really the same, Camille? It sure as hell doesn't sound like it to me. Of course, I'm not really sure what you're talking about. It's all a bit encrypted."

She shrugged. "Yes, they are the same. People were unintendedly hurt by words spoken."

Hunt saw pain reflected in Camille's watery eyes now and it bothered him it was there. "Who upset you with... how did you say it, unpleasant things said about you?" She looked at him but didn't answer. "I can see the pain in your eyes, Camille. Who was it? Your mother? Your father?" Her eyes fluttered when he'd mentioned her father. "Ah. It is your father. I can see the sadness and pain in your eyes from it. I feel it pulsing off of you, sweetheart. Tell me what happened. It may lessen your pain if you share it with me."

A tear slid down her cheek. She shook her head and he knew she wasn't going to tell him. "You feel too much already." She wiped the tears away. "I believe you have a special gift to understand a person's soul, Hunt." She sucked in a deep breath. "I wish you didn't see and understand so much."

He leaned back. "Me too."

"But you don't understand all of it. You see the feelings. Pain, hope, joy, fear, love. You can't always know how those feelings were born, nurtured, and destroyed." She stood. "For your sanity and peace of mind, I don't want you to know those things as you look through the camera lens. It's already too much of a burden for one man to bear to see what you see. You deserve your peace and your place of respite." She faced him and he stood. "I

won't ever be the person who robs you of your peace...I..."
She shook her head, not wanting to finish the sentence.

He knew she was going to tell him that she loved him.
He also knew that she felt it was best for him to not know
it. His chest hurt, seeing her walk away and stand alone at
the bow of the boat. Should he follow her? She'd told him
why she'd left Fa La La a year ago – to let the dust settle
over the dissolution of other people's dreams for her and
another man. They weren't her true dreams, but she'd let
the community make them hers for a long time. Was that
still what was driving her away? Should he delve into it
further? Should he try to convince her to stay?

Crap. He ran his hands through his hair. She was a
smart woman who made critical decisions that meant life
or death for a person. Shouldn't he trust her with making
decisions for her own life? She was leaving Fa La La. That
left him, who was trying to make a new life for himself on
Cypress Island, possibly only seeing her at Christmas and
an occasional meet-up in New York if he was traveling
through. They'd had one exceptional rainy afternoon
together under the tin roof of an old lopsided cabin, when
the world went away and he enjoyed the absolute
harmony and peace of being with the sun.

His heart ached more and more with each step he
took moving away from her. He looked up at the
wheelhouse and saw June. She was resting her head on T-
Dud's chest. He had his arm around her. When she saw
Hunt looking at her, her eyes widened – almost in a plea.
A plea for what? What did she want with him, the man
that was ruining her village, her way of life, so he could
have his own? T-Dud looked at his wife and followed
where she was looking. His proud shoulders dropped. He
spoke to June and she took the wheel of the boat. Hunt
moved toward the wheelhouse door, knowing T-Dud was
coming to speak to him.

"I've got eyes and June has enough power to get me to
act on what I see," T-Dud said, his tone a little angry.
"Youz should know what I just found out." He swallowed

hard. "Let's walk to the back of the boat." When they got as far from Camille as possible, he continued. "Youz are a stubborn man, who cares more about himself than his neighbors, but Camille sees something in you—so does June. I guess, if I wasn't too ticked off at you to admit it, I do too." No, it wasn't anger, Hunt realized. It was pride. "I hurt my *bebette*. I said something I shouldn't have. June thinks you should know. She said you care about my daughter. Is that true?"

"Yes. Very much so. But before you say something personal you might regret—you should know, Camille's leaving Fa La La. No matter what you tell me, I have no say in that. I wouldn't try to tell her what to do either. I think too much of that has been done."

T-Dud nodded. "Fair enough." He proceeded to tell Hunt anyway.

Chapter Eight

"This came from your thumb," Camille said, handing a storage bag with a fish hook inside to a very brave six-year-old little boy sitting cross-legged on the narrow ER treatment bed, in the recently renovated ER at Bayou Regional Hospital. "Next time I see you, I hope you're handing me a storage bag with fish in it that you caught."

"I will. I promise," he said, his eyes big and bright as he studied the hook.

Camille walked out of the room, and down the short hall with its highly polished gray floor to the brightly lit shared ER physician's office. It was laid out a lot like the wheelhouse of a trawl boat. She sat at the huge desk and stared at the large computer monitor in front of her, not really seeing anything. She wished she didn't feel anything either.

Trying to cope with the decisions she'd made now and almost a year ago was why she'd said yes to the CEO of the Bayou Regional Hospital in Cane, who'd called late the night before to ask her to help him get out of a bind. He needed a board-certified ER physician the next morning to cover a twelve-hour shift. Since he and many of the administrative staff had helped her with between-semester jobs, reference letters, and scholarships to help pay for her costly medical tuition, she couldn't refuse him. Besides, it was best that she spent a full day away from Fa La La and Hunt.

Especially Hunt.

Through his amazing photography, his actions, and his words, he'd exposed who he was to Camille. It was why, in the short time they'd known each other, she'd fallen in love with him. But walking away from him in order to give him what he needed was the hardest thing she'd ever had to do in her life. And she'd had to do some pretty hard things. She wanted to be with him, to love him, laugh with him, share her life with him. But because she truly loved him, what she wanted didn't factor in. When he'd said he needed peace to survive, she believed him. She understood it because she understood him. He needed what he got from Cypress Island being his home.

And, the people of Fa La La needed their homes too. Whose survival was more important? Camille couldn't answer that. As a physician she'd always tried to save everyone, not having to make the call on who lived and who died. She'd tried to do the same here, once she knew what she was dealing with. But it was an impossible situation.

Save Fa La La or save Hunt.

What she could decide was what she had to do to get through her pain from leaving Fa La La again and from leaving Hunt. Since she'd returned, she'd rediscovered all of the reasons she loved her childhood home. Sharing the traditions, the people, and the history with Hunt had given her that gift. She hadn't resolved all of the things that sent her away, but leaving her family was breaking her heart almost as much as walking away from the man she loved.

Almost.

Camille pressed her hand to the ache in her chest. She wondered if her next painful breath was going to crush her ribs. When patients wound up in front of her claiming they were dying of a broken heart, she attributed their symptoms to anxiety, depression, spasms from crying too hard, but not a broken heart. Now, she understood.

"Dr. Comeaux, you have a patient in treatment room one," a nurse's voice told her over the intercom. Camille looked at the digital clock on the wall. One hour before her shift was over.

"Well, it took you long enough," Tante Pearl said in Cajun French, when Camille walked through the soft green curtain inside the enclosed glass room. But, it wasn't Tante Pearl who was there for medical attention. She was sitting in the visitor's hard plastic chair. It was Hunter. Her heart slammed against her chest. She quickly went to him, pulling on her exam gloves.

"Hello, Camille," he said, a crooked grin on his face.

She swallowed hard. *He's okay,* she told herself. He wasn't in the critical care or the trauma suite. And he was sitting upright, with his legs hanging off the table. But there was blood on the collar of his tan shirt, a lot of it. She immediately started looking at his skull. "What happened, Hunt?"

"I had a run-in with a broom."

"He didn't have no run-in. I cracked it over his head," Tante Pearl said in broken English. She pushed up her black, cat's-eye glasses and folded her arms over her pale green housedress with hollies on it. "I'd do it again, too. Only I'd use the mop and not take a chance to ruin my good broom on his hard head."

Camille looked at Hunt and saw the twinkle in his eyes, despite his injury. Her heart thudded hard in her chest. She had to stay away from him, it was just too hard to have such strong feelings and know he was off-limits. She moved a little closer to him to tend to his wound and his fresh, his clean scent wafted to her. He smelled like the crisp, cotton duvet where they'd made love. "Why did you hit him with your broom, Tante Pearl?"

"Oh, c'est rascal." She looked at Hunt and frowned, but Camille saw something else in her expression too. She wasn't as angry as she pretended to be.

"Truth is, Doc," he said, smiling at Camille. "I tried to steal a kiss from her. Someone told me if a girl stands under the mistletoe, she can't deny a fella a kiss."

"See, what I tole you." She nodded.

Camille laughed. Even with her heart in a battle with loving this man and resisting him, he still could make her laugh. "I need to close that up." She stepped out and spoke to a nurse, who followed her back in with the staple kit and injection.

"Oh, no," Tante Pearl, fretted. "This ain't good. Oh no."

"The good news is: I don't have to shave your hair. Bad news is you'll need three staples. I recommend getting the local to numb it."

"I trust you with my life, Camille. Do what you think is best."

She looked at him, the syringe in her hand. Dear Lord, she wanted to kiss this man, hold him, love him. No. Her decision had been a good one. She quickly did her job and closed his wound. She was checking her work, when the door opened.

"Knock. Knock. Knock," Pierre said, just inside the door, but behind the curtain. "How's the patient?"

"He broke my broom," Tante Pearl said in English.

Pierre walked in and Hunt started laughing. "Well, I'll be damned," he said, looking at Pierre from head to toe.

Pearl made the sign of the cross. "Watch your language."

"Navy dress slacks and blue shirt? An expensive silk tie?" Hunter shook his head. "You're a fraud?" Mostly. He still had a long, strawberry blonde ponytail, now neatly combed and pulled back tightly.

"No, I'm CEO of Bayou Regional Hospital. I also grew up in Fa La La. I inherited my father's boat and enjoy using it when I can." He kissed Tante Pearl on the cheek. "I'm buying you a padded broom so you don't hurt anyone else."

"You're discharged, Hunt." She started to shake his hand as she did with all of her patients, but caught herself before she reached for his hand. He wasn't like any of her other patients. To touch Hunt again would be a temptation beyond any she'd had to face in her life. She signed the chart and handed it to the nurse who walked in.

Pierre immediately gave Camille a heavy manila envelope and lowered his voice for just her to hear. "I don't need to know right now. Monday will be fine."

She opened the large envelope, responding in hushed tones as Pierre had. "An employment contract? You want to hire me?"

"Hell, yeah. I need you. It's not easy getting doctors to work at smaller hospitals, even regional hospitals." He tapped the folder. "Your family wants you here." He shrugged. "What more can a person ask for—oh, money. You'll see that's in there too."

"But I have a job in..."

"In the contract. We'll negotiate and pay, within reason, to release you from that employment agreement." He walked to the door. "See you."

Camille walked out of the hospital, still in her scrubs, but now wearing her UGGS instead of her work tennis shoes. Hunt was standing next to a black Range Rover in the spot where she'd parked her momma's car. "I assume you had something to do with why the car is missing and I don't have to call 911."

He nodded. "You might still have to make that call, if you don't get in the car P-D-Q." He grimaced and hiked his thumb toward the car. "Tante Pearl said her blood sugar is low and she needs to eat a praline or she's going to turn into a rougarou. Whatever that is. It sounds 911 worthy."

Camille laughed and her heart broke a little bit more. No one made her laugh like Hunt did. She'd miss his sense of humor if she went back to New York, which she knew she should do. "Rougarou is a Cajun werewolf."

"Yikes." His eyes widened and his mouth pulled tight as he pretended to be frightened. He looked into the backseat of his SUV. "No fur on her face or arms yet. We'd better hurry."

Camille climbed into the front seat and he drove toward the Cane boat launch not that far away. "How's your head?"

"Fine."

"She's threatened all of us with that broom for decades. This is the first time she ever actually followed through."

"My lucky day." He motioned to Tante Pearl in the back seat. "Is that her snoring or is her inner werewolf coming out?"

Camille glanced at her aunt but her thoughts turned to the conversation she had to have with Hunt. She looked at him and his smile faded. "I think we should just say good-bye now," she said, her throat tightening. "My flight's Monday morning, but I'm thinking of spending a day in New Orleans before I leave."

She couldn't bear seeing him again tomorrow. She looked out the window, surprised they were already at the boat launch parking lot. Camille was both glad for it and sad.

"Momma and Papa are here to get us?" she said surprised, seeing them standing on the wharf.

Hunt walked to her door and opened it. He leaned inside. "I'm not saying good-bye, but I'll take a kiss." He reached in his pocket and pulled a small cluster of mistletoe leaves over her head. She sucked in a breath.

"You don't know what you're asking of me."

"I sure the hell do." He grabbed the back of her head and lightly kissed her mouth like she was as fragile as spun sugar. She tried to remember everything she could about this long, beautiful final kiss – the texture of his full bottom lip, the pressure of his smooth tongue, the heated mingling of their breaths...

A hand flew from the back of the car and smacked Hunt in the head. He jerked up and hit his head on the ceiling of the car. "Son of a..." he bit the final word, out of respect for a woman who'd smacked him on the wound she'd given him. He waved the mistletoe for her to see.

"Mon Dieu." She opened the door and stormed away toward the boat.

Camille started laughing. "I'm sorry. I shouldn't laugh. Let me look at your head."

"I'm fine." He motioned to her parents, still waiting on the dock. "Go on. Talk to your parents. I'll be right behind you."

She took a deep fortifying breath to calm her nerves as she walked on board and into the wheelhouse as Hunt released the lines and climbed on board. He remained on deck, while Tante Pearl stayed in the wheelhouse where she could sit securely and warmly. Camille spoke freely in front of her great-aunt, and so did her parents. They trusted her to not judge and to not repeat what was said during the twenty-minutes ride to Fa La La.

"I'm sorry," her papa said, tears in his eyes. "I'm ashamed of not always trustin' you. I shouldn't have ever thought or said what I did dat night before you left. I had no idea you heard me. Youz momma only tole me because Hunt said she needed to. I'm so sorry."

"Hunt? How did he know Momma knew I was there? I didn't know." Camille thought of the last night she was in Fa La La before she moved away. She'd come to her parent's house to visit after work. Her mother and papa were in the kitchen having coffee and cake, talking. They didn't know she was there, as they kept speaking to one another about her. Her papa was blaming her for Ben falling in love with another woman and for being too picky to settle for another man. Her heart had broken, little by little with each word he spoke. Then, when he'd said she'd chased Ben away with her cold, uncaring, selfish behavior for reasons he didn't understand after he'd already fallen in love with the grand-babies he imagined they'd have, her heart split in two. Her momma must've heard her leave then and never said anything about it.

Why hadn't she?

Now, over a year later the three of them were talking about it. Her momma explained she felt it was Camille that needed to speak of it when she was ready and that if she'd told T-Dud before then that his daughter had heard him, he wouldn't wait for when she was ready. Her wise loving momma had given her the space she needed. Her papa's eyes were bright with unshed tears as he described his hurtful words about her as "unforgivable'. Yet as they neared Fa La La, she forgave him. He'd explained to her how he'd met Ben's fiancé, Elli, that day and liked her. The day her papa had uttered those words in confidence to his wife, was the day that he had given up on his dreams for her marrying the man he'd loved as a son and had already considered a son-in-law although neither Camille nor Ben said that would be so.

Camille accepted her papa's apology and asked her parents to forgive her for not thinking about their feelings through all of this, too. She could see by their expressions that she was, indeed, forgiven and still deeply loved.

Relief swept through her. They'd turned the corner of their relationship.

Hunt opened the wheelhouse door and waved for her to come outside. "My turn." He escorted her to the bow of the boat.

"My parents told me that you set up this time for them to talk to me. Thank you for your role in this, Hunt, I ..." He placed his finger over her lips.

"I want to talk about us. Take a walk with me." He turned, and waved his hands over his head. There was a loud snap, then his island went from complete darkness to light.

"Oh, my..." She didn't know where to look first. Lights were strung in cypress trees along the water's edge and even on his lopsided cabin. "It's all there," she whispered, spotting the lover's path, the Kissing Bough-mistletoe gazebo, the live reindeer in a fenced area, and even the painted cypress-knee village near the wharf. She clapped her hands. "You did this?"

He shook his head. "Your family deserves the credit. They worked so hard to have this completed for you before you leave to go back to New York. They wanted to let you know how much they love you and appreciate you."

"You allowed it."

They got off the boat and walked onto the island. Hunt didn't seem to be enjoying the wonderland as much as she did. His shoulders were tense, his brows tight. She was about to ask him if he was sorry for allowing his island to be decorated, but they started to stroll along lover's lane, and she felt it wasn't the right time to do it.

"Deck the Halls" started to play in the background.

They turned at a corner where a beautiful Christmas tree had been decorated with twinkling white lights, wide white ribbons, and a brightly shining angel on top. The angel was wearing sunglasses. Hunt took the sunglasses off and slipped them on her face. "You need these more." He smiled. "These are better than using your hands to shade your eyes."

"I forgot mine on the plane when I flew here." She laughed.

The path disappeared behind a grove of palmettos, where the light dimmed to just light the path.

"You asked me if a place could give me peace, Camille. Remember?"

"I remember," she said, her heart now pounding in her chest.

"Tante Izzy told me last night that I didn't choose this island, it chose me." He was quiet a moment. She could see in the intensity of his eyes that what he wanted to say was very important to him. "She also said I didn't own it, I was its guardian and with that I had some responsibilities."

"That's what gave you this change of heart, then," she said, happy for him.

He stopped in front of the small white gazebo where a beautifully decorated Kissing Bough hung in the center. There were huge branches of mistletoe, cedar, rosemary, and mint. Mixed in were pecans, navel oranges, and gold ribbon. He took her hand and stood a foot away from being underneath it.

He turned and faced her. "I have had a change of heart, Camille. But it had nothing to do with what Tante Izzy said. It had to do with who you are. From the moment I saw you on your water chariot the day you arrived here, I felt your peace. Yes, it's true, I came to Louisiana thinking Cypress Island was where I'd find my peace and I was right. This is where I found you. I'm so in love with you, Camille, in what seems a crazy short period of time, but I am. The island may have chosen me, but my heart chose you. I'm asking you now...Do you choose me?"

Camille looked into his warm, beautiful eyes, and a peace she didn't know she was seeking seeped into her heart and soul. She sucked in a breath, and she saw that Hunt was perspiring around the edges of his dark hair. She took his hand and pulled him under the mistletoe.

"I choose you." She stood on her toes and kissed him. "And, I choose to be home here in Fa La La."

He picked her up and spun her around as the chorus sounded on the speakers through the trees-*'Tis the season to be jolly, Fa la la la la, la la la la*

Dear Reader,

I hope you enjoyed *Hunt for Christmas*. It was such a pleasure to write this story for you as part of the Under the Kissing Bough collection. I truly loved sharing some of the Christmas traditions that we celebrate with our families in Cajun Country in this work of fiction. If you'd like to add a bit of Cajun Holiday cheer with your family, visit my website - tinadesalvo.com for some yummy recipes that have been passed on for generations (including the pecan pralines prepared by Tante Izzy and Madame Eleanor in the story).

I wish you and your family a very Merry Christmas and plenty of kisses Under the Kissing Bough!

Joyeaux Noel,

Tina DeSalvo

P.S. *Hunt for Christmas* is part of my Second Chance Novel Series where some of the same characters you've gotten to know, appear again in stories of romance, warmth and fun. Learn more about these other stories at tinadesalvo.com

Gateau De Sirop

Syrup Cake

A Christmas favorite for many Cajun families!

1 large egg
1 cup cane syrup
1 teaspoon baking soda
2 cups all purpose flour
1 cup boiling water
2 tablespoons butter

In a bowl beat the egg; add syrup and flour, mix well (this is the cake mixture). Preheat the oven at 350 degrees. Put butter in the pan (7x11x2), melt it in the oven. Once it is melted, spread the butter in the pan (including sidewalls). Add baking soda to boiling water − be careful to hold the cup of boiling water over a bowl when the soda is added as it bubbles over. Add the well-blended baking soda and boiling water to the cake mixture. Mix and pour into the pan. Cover it with pecans, then bake for 20 minutes. Serve warm with whipped cream or plain. My mother-in-law, Gloria, says it's easy to make and delicious.

Oyster Dressing

Everyone living down the bayou knows that oysters taste best in months ending in "r". One way to enjoy oysters is in an oyster dressing for Thanksgiving (November) and Christmas (December).

4 pints fresh oysters, drained and coarsely chopped,
    reserve the liquid
1 stick of butter
The Trinity: 3 medium bell peppers chopped
              3 stalks of celery finely diced
              2 medium onions chopped
1   bunch green onions (scallions)
1/4 cup minced garlic
2   loaves of French bread, crumbled
4   ounces Parmesan Cheese
2   cups plain bread crumbs
Fresh parsley chopped
1   tbsp cayenne pepper
2   tbsp white pepper
Salt to taste

Sauté the vegetables in butter until soft. Add the oysters and continue sautéing for 4-5 minutes. Add the reserved oyster liquid. Add the crumbled bread, cayenne pepper and white pepper. Mix well. If the dressing seems too wet and soggy (remember it will be baked), add the plain breadcrumbs as needed. Spread the mixture into a 13x9-baking pan and add cheese. Bake for 15-20 minutes at 350 degrees.

For more recipes visit tinadesalvo.com

Coming in 2017

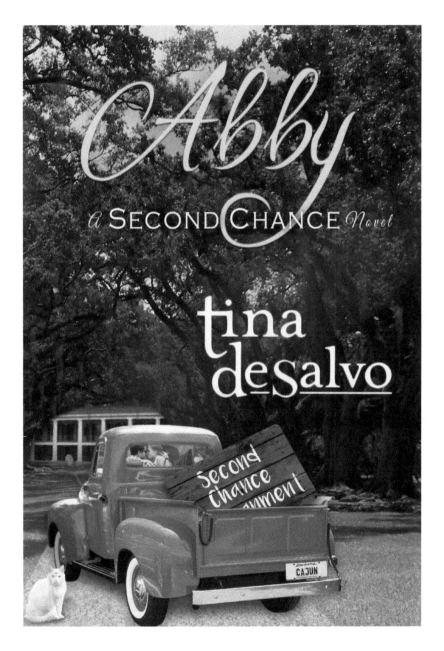

Abby

a SECOND CHANCE *Novel*

tina deSalvo